The Honeymoon Homicides

A Provincetown Mystery

Jeannette de Beauvoir

The Honeymoon Homicides: A Provincetown Mystery
Copyright © 2024 by Jeannette de Beauvoir

Published by HomePort Press
PO Box 1508
Provincetown, MA 02657
www.HomePortPress.com

ISBN   979-8-9868654-3-0
eISBN 979-8-9868654-4-7

Cover Design by Miladinka Milic

The Honeymoon Homicides is a work of fiction. Other than those individuals who have given their permission and certain well-known landmarks, all names, characters, places, situations, and incidents are the products of the author's imagination and used fictitiously. Any other resemblance to actual events, or persons, living or dead, is purely coincidental.

Also by Jeannette de Beauvoir

Mysteries:
Sydney Riley series:
> *Death of. Bear*
> *Murder at Fantasia Fair*
> *The Deadliest Blessing*
> *A Killer Carnival*
> *A Fatal Folly*
> *The Matinée Murders*
> *The Lethal Legacy*
> *The Fine Art of Deception*

Martine LeDuc series:
> *Asylum*
> *Deadly Jewels*
> *Trapped*

Trinity Pierce series:
> *Murder Most Academic* (as Alicia Stone)

Historical Fiction:
> *Our Lady of the Dunes*
> *Lethal Alliances*

1

The victim generously waited to be murdered until the final vows had been spoken and we were officially declared married. And that's pretty much the best thing I can say about my wedding.

Not that it hadn't begun auspiciously. I used to be wedding coordinator at Provincetown's Race Point Inn—of which I was now co-owner—and so I had considerable experience wrangling vendors, petulant family members, and weather forecasts. And my partner Ali and I had reached an uneasy compromise with my mother in terms of the size and lavishness of the affair—no small feat, as my mother is abnormally addicted to big weddings. We were in addition juggling two religions and two cultures, as Ali is Muslim and his parents and extended family are all Lebanese. And we had somehow navigated all that.

What we hadn't reckoned with, of course, was the body falling through the awning onto the terrace and, of course, the screams that followed.

***

"Sydney, you are not going to make this stop you," was what Mirela said.

"Stop me from doing what?" I probably sounded distracted, mainly because I was distracted. The police, in the persons of a bunch of uniformed officers and my sometimes-sort-of-friend Julie Agassi, who was the head of Provincetown's small detective unit, were swarming all over the place, putting up tape and directing people away from the immediate area. The rescue squad was there, too, though what they thought they could do to help a man who seemed to have broken every bone in his body and spread a great deal of his viscera around the patio was unknown. The wedding guests, in various stages of shock and occasional hysteria, had allowed themselves to be herded into the inn's restaurant, already set up for the wedding dinner.

My mother was demanding loudly how such a thing could have been allowed and asking about suing the owners, apparently forgetting for the moment that I was one of them. My newly minted husband, Ali, was dealing with his parents, who'd seen more than enough of this kind of violence before they'd permanently fled Beirut and were dealing with some sort of PTSD shock.

And now my best friend Mirela was giving me… what? A pep talk?

"You should go now," she said. "Leave for the honeymoon. You and Ali. There is no dinner. There is no dancing."

"We weren't doing dancing anyway," I said blankly. After the initial shock, it was dawning on me that I was standing twenty feet from a corpse, wearing a bloodied wedding gown, and realizing—priorities being priorities—that I was not going to have, after all, a wedding feast catered by Adrienne the diva chef, who kept our restaurant's Michelin stars intact and who has made P'town a destination for world-class dining. "This," I said to Mirela, "is the worst wedding I've ever planned."

She tossed the blonde hair escaping from her up-do—not that she looked any less gorgeous a little bedraggled—and peered at me. "Are you feeling all right?"

"No," I said.

She took my elbow and turned me away from the scene unfolding on the terrace. "What you need," she said firmly, "is a drink."

"What I need is fourteen drinks," I said. "But I should check on my mother—"

"The last thing you do is check on your mother," she said. Mirela and my mother are not what you might call simpatico, mostly due to my mother's criticisms of Mirela's single status and her underappreciation of Mirela's art (which earned her grudging respect only when she learned that the work routinely sold in the six-figure range).

"It doesn't look like anything," was her response to the abstract paintings that were now exhibited worldwide, and, "I don't understand why she can't find a husband."

Mirela steered me to the bar area, already filling up with wedding guests in various stages of shock and all, apparently, requiring alcohol. She caught the bartender's eye—a skill all the Bulgarians I've ever met have perfected—and he uncorked a bottle of wine and handed it across to her. She grabbed it without letting go of my elbow, and pulled me out of the restaurant and over to the small lounge area that had the advantage of having a door, which she closed behind us right away. "Here," she said, handing me the bottle, and rooting around in a cupboard for a glass.

I was looking at the label in some dismay. "This is Châteauneuf-du-Pape," I protested.

"Of course it is." Her voice was brisk. "You need a drink."

"A deplorable reason to drink *this*," I insisted. It's my favorite wine ever.

"Even more deplorable, sunshine," said Mirela, "is that your guests will drink it if you do not."

I sat down on the couch. I was understanding what romance writers were talking about when they used terms like "crumple." I took a swig of wine straight out of the bottle, heaping blasphemy on blasphemy. "Where's Ali?"

"He will find us." She gave up trying to locate a glass and slanted a look over. "You are regaining color," she informed me.

Which was more than we could say about the fellow out on the inn's patio.

When the door opened, it wasn't Ali standing there, but Julie, officious and sharp, her blonde hair and blue eyes making her look, always, like some kind of ice princess. "I *thought* you might be hiding somewhere," she said.

I gave a weak gesture with the wine bottle. "Join the party," I said.

She narrowed her eyes. "Are you drunk?"

"Not yet."

"Then hold off." She half-turned and spoke to someone behind her, and another cop came in, pulling the door closed behind him. He looked around the room, fast, the way cops do when they go anywhere, and found a straight chair and pulled out a notebook.

I know about what cops do. My husband is one of them. "It's an odd word, isn't it, husband?" I said. "Sounds sort of like a thump."

Julie ignored me and said to the uniform, "Interview Sydney Riley, eight-fifteen pm." She sat on a chair she pulled over close to the couch, snapping her fingers in front of my face. "Focus, Sydney," she said.

I sighed and put the bottle on the floor. Not too far away, just in case.

She still wasn't sure of me. "Can you go find Ali?" Julie asked Mirela, who nodded and slipped out the door. Even Mirela knows not to argue with her. "Tell us what happened here," said Julie.

I was having some trouble focusing on her. How can you feel drunk on one swig of wine? "I got married," I said. "Somebody died." I paused. "Who was he?"

"Not one of your wedding guests," Julie said, almost absently. She was looking at a list, probably supplied by Mike, the Race Point Inn's co-owner. He's frighteningly competent. "Unless he was a last-minute addition? Do you know someone named Barclay Cargill?"

"That can't be a real name," I said automatically, then realized she was serious. "No. No, I've never heard of him."

"He was staying at your inn."

I stared at her. "We have eighty rooms," I said. "I'm not the manager. You really think I know everybody?"

"You may remember him." She produced her iPhone, flipped around a bit, then extended it to me. The man in the photo had dark hair and a beard that were starting to turn gray; what was most remarkable was that he was wearing a three-piece suit. People in P'town don't wear three-piece suits.

Some people in P'town don't wear much at all.

Julie retrieved her phone. "He's an attorney," she said.

She'd gotten her information remarkably quickly. "Okay," I said. "So did he jump, or was he pushed?"

She was unamused. "You're being remarkably flippant about someone's violent death."

"I'm remarkably flippant about anyone who gets murdered in the middle of my wedding." I plucked at my ivory lace overskirt. "Just thought I'd remind you, in case you thought I was wearing this for a costume party. If he weren't already dead, my mother would have killed him by now."

She sighed. Julie sighs a lot when she's around me. She's even been known to refer to me as Provincetown's answer to Miss Marple, and she doesn't mean that in a good way.

It's not exactly my fault that when someone gets murdered I end up having something to do with figuring it out. Julie thinks there's some sort of cause and effect, but there really isn't. I just know a lot of people—and it's a small town.

But having a murder committed during my *wedding*? That was taking this whole amateur sleuthing thing just a little too far.

As though reading my thoughts, Julie said, "All right. You don't know this man. Good. Can I take it that you won't be trying to figure out what happened to him?"

The events of the past hour were starting to turn nasty on me, and I really wanted to be with Ali, not Julie. "No more than you are," I said sweetly. It was a jab, of course: in Massachusetts, possible homicides are investigated by the state police, not the local force. I knew it was a sore spot with Julie, who thinks she's better at it than they are. She can secure the scene, take preliminary statements, and assist the Staties when they arrive. "Is that all? Because—"

The door swung open and I've never, I think, been happier to see anyone. "Are you all right?" asked Ali. He didn't even wait for me to respond. "She can give her statement later," he said to Julie.

"She needs to do it while it's fresh in her mind," Julie said.

"Like most of our guests, she didn't see anything until the individual was already on the ground," said Ali. "She doesn't need this now."

"Maybe you two could stop talking about me like I'm not here?" I asked, my voice sharper than I'd meant it to be. Ali came and sat beside me, carefully moving the bottle of Châteauneuf aside so he wouldn't knock it over. He knew I'd need it later; it wasn't exactly an occasion for Champagne, despite all the Veuve Clicquot that Martin, the maître d', had waiting for us on ice.

Not that Ali drank alcohol, anyway.

I slid my hand into his; for all my rather aggressive petulance, I was feeling a little lost and a little sad. It was finally dawning on me that someone had died. At my inn. At my wedding.

Ali looked, of course, wonderful. He annoyingly always does. He has beautiful dark eyes and beautiful olive skin and dark hair that curls ever so slightly and is always just a little too long, and designer stubble that makes him look sexy and a little dangerous.

Well, he *is* an agent for Immigration and Customs Enforcement. The danger is real.

Julie was giving up. She jerked her head towards the other cop, who closed his notebook, stood up, and left the room. "You may be needed later on," she said to me. "Both of you, in fact. Should the *state police* have any questions about the individual." Oh, yeah, I'd hit a nerve.

I liked that business about the "individual." I'd come way too close to saying something about him crashing the party. It must have been the shock; I hadn't had nearly enough wine to account for it.

"We're leaving in the morning," I said.

"You can't—" she started, automatically, and I interrupted her. "Honeymoon," I said firmly.

"We'll be back next week," said Ali.

Even Julie Agassi knows when she's beaten. She gave us one last stern official look, and fled.

"Well," said Ali, putting his arm around my shoulder. "How do you like married life so far?"

2

Provincetown, my home, is a place that reaches out—almost hopefully—into the Atlantic Ocean before curling back on itself, a spiral that sets us apart from ocean and land alike. It's a foothold of sand that's always moving, and we go to sleep and awaken to the sound of waves.

We're called Land's End, primarily because no one gets here by accident—the next stop is Portugal. We're in a liminal space that blurs the distinction between land and water, and things happen here that don't happen anywhere else.

For centuries this part of the Cape was also referred to as the graveyard of the Atlantic, due to the number of shipwrecks caused by those waves and those treacherous shifting sands— in the eighteenth and nineteenth centuries, they averaged two wrecks a month in winter. These days, the Cape Cod Canal allows shipping to avoid our coast; but there isn't a year when there's suddenly part of some ancient tragedy or other surfacing.

And while other treacherous shorelines were known for their "mooncussers"—people who deliberately shut down lighthouses and put up other lights to lure ships onto sand or rocks—Cape Cod pillagers were contented in large measure to wait for ships to wreck themselves… and they never had long to wait.

The first "coast guards" were volunteers who walked these beaches in patrols of two, watching uneasily for a wreck so they could summon help. It was a dangerous job; their exceedingly cheerful motto was, "You have to go, but you don't have to come back." And as the weather wasn't conducive to hanging out on the beach, they eventually grabbed wood from the wrecks and fashioned huts with a dual purpose: to shelter sailors who managed to get ashore from a wreck (only to freeze once they got there), and to keep the coastal guardians from the elements when they weren't on patrol.

Eventually Congress established the US Life-Saving Service and stations were built at Race Point and Peaked Hill and seven other places on the Cape; but many of the old dune shacks, as they were by then called, remained and were adapted by families with names as old as P'town itself: Tasha, Malicoat, Santos.

Then, in the heady summer of 1916, when a world war made it impossible for the Bohemian arts intelligentsia of Greenwich Village to make its annual pilgrimage to Paris, artists and writers flocked to Provincetown instead, many of them finding solace and inspiration out in the dunes. Eugene O'Neill lived in one of the dune shacks while he wrote *Beyond the Horizon*.

And thus an art colony was established, as decades passed and the shacks continued to shelter (mostly summers only, as there was no heat, no electricity, no running water, though there were some hardy souls who endured year-round) artists and poets and eccentrics, along with the original families who continued the upkeep on their shacks. Eventually a handful of the buildings became the responsibility of two nonprofits, which granted fellowship stays to visual artists and writers and protected and maintained the shacks in the off-season.

One of the best things that happened to Cape Cod was the establishment of the Seashore as a national park; if that hadn't happened, we'd have had developers building mansions right up to the shore, and there wouldn't be places like Race Point and Herring Cove and Beech Forest for everyone to explore and enjoy. The dune shacks, however, presented a problem. The National Seashore would have preferred for them all to disappear and nature to reclaim the dunes, but there was an uneasy détente until 2012, when families and organizations that had been pressing for the shacks to be declared a historic district were finally granted that distinction. Owned by the Seashore, the shacks were granted leases lasting decades.

In their efforts to introduce people to life in the dunes, a few of the shacks offer week-long stays to community members who enter a yearly lottery, and as it happened, my co-owner, Mike, had won the lottery—and promptly made it his wedding gift to me and Ali. A week in a dune shack. Not everyone's romantic cup of tea—and I'd be lying if I said I hadn't had passing thoughts of Paris or Singapore—but even I had to admit that a week away from humanity wasn't such a bad thing.

Martin the maître d' had supervised the packing of food—we had to be self-sufficient for a week—while my mother had assembled a list of reasons why a week in a shack with no electricity and no running water was not the honeymoon she'd expected for her daughter. (Once I'd acidly pointed out that my first marriage—to a surgeon, no less, she'd been over the moon about *that*—had included a honeymoon to Rio, and we'd still gotten divorced, she decided—independently, of course—to discontinue the list.)

The consortium's big old station wagon drove us in and struggled once or twice on the sand, but we made it all right and were dropped off after a brief introduction to the outhouse ("put popcorn down it once a week"), the small propane-powered stove and even smaller refrigerator, and a demonstration of how to pump water, which I have to say takes more strength than one might at first think.

The shacks surprise you, appearing where nothing had been at first glance, clinging organically to the sand or standing oddly and majestically separate from it on stilts; some of them barely noticeable, others obvious, silhouetted against the sea. They were all baking under the hot sun, pressed down into the sand until they seemed to be part of it.

We stood and watched the car lumbering on its way, a little as though we were Scott watching the Antarctic expedition leave with little hope of return, and Ali slid his arms around me; he was almost tall enough to rest his chin on my head. "So, *cara*, here we are at last," he said. He thinks speaking Italian is sexy. He's right, though I'd never tell him so.

"Here we are," I agreed.

The sun was high and everything seemed sharp, over-bright, tinged with something disquieting I couldn't quite put my finger on. I smiled, dismissed it, and turned to face my new husband, slipping my arms around him in turn. He was wearing jeans with holes at the knees, a t-shirt that said *How Does It Feel to be a Problem?* (a honeymoon gift from his sister Karen, who wore hijab and was quick to remind him of his Arabic background), and he'd kicked off his shoes.

He looked delicious. "I don't suppose," I said, as diffidently as I could manage, "We could try that consummation thing again? Make sure we got it right last night?"

He raised his eyebrows. "In the middle of the day in a ramshackle hut on the edge of the Atlantic Ocean?"

"Well, now that you put it that way, yes."

"Sounds like a plan."

Later, with Ali negotiating the workings of his brand-new fishing pole, I went for a walk.

I didn't feel ready to unpack, or think about meals or sleep or anything; I didn't even feel fully present to my honeymoon, which has to be a terrible thing, with the weight—no pun intended—of the body that had interrupted my wedding still very much in my consciousness.

I had a feeling he wasn't going away that easily, that dead lawyer. But not today.

They're an odd group, these shacks, eclectic in design–some on stilts, while others nestle into the very side of a dune, with only the roof visible–and yet they all have one thing in common: in their desire for privacy, they have been built so that none of them looks directly into another. The hills created by the dunes were used to great advantage; you could be close to a shack and yet barely be able to tell if it was inhabited or not.

I bumped into one of them, literally, coming round a dune and suddenly there the shack was, rising abruptly out of the lee of the hill, and a wizened man peering crossly out at me from its shadows. The shack was surrounded by little flat square boxes on poles, at least twenty or thirty of them, and the air was humming with the flights of birds, flitting in and out of them. I gasped in delight, and his expression lightened. "They're beautiful!" I exclaimed.

His face creased into a smile.

"What are they?" I asked, curious about the birds, yeah, but also about one of the backshore's eccentrics.

"Tree swallows," he said, and his voice sounded creaky, as though he wasn't accustomed to using it.

The birds were fast and deft, whizzing around and diving into the small holes cut into the birdhouses, from which emanated the sounds of cries—babies being fed, no doubt. I watched them for a moment, then watched him, too, his face creased with a permanent smile of affection. "My name's Sydney Riley," I said, a little impulsively, not sure whether he cared.

He nodded without looking at me. "Happen yer stayin' at Louis's shack," he said.

"Louis?"

"Name of fellow built it. Back before the war. They call it something new and shiny these days, but it's Louis's shack."

"Who was Louis?"

He finally turned to look at me. "Miss Riley," he said, "maybe it's best if you don't find out."

***

Ali came back, disgruntled, with nothing to show for his afternoon but a slight sunburn. "What did you expect, your first try?" I asked.

"I expected," he said, mopping sweat from his forehead, "to bring home something big and luscious for dinner."

"Just as well you didn't." I shrugged and continued inventorying what could fit into the tiny fridge.

"Why?"

"Because neither of us would know what to do with it."

"There's that," he conceded, stowing the pole and bucket on the porch and closing the screen door firmly behind him; we'd already noted the mosquitoes and sand flies that had us in mind for *their* supper.

"Anyway, Mirela sent *shopska* salad and meatball soup, so we won't starve."

He perked up right away. "And *banitsa?*" Ali makes up for not drinking alcohol by having a prodigious sweet tooth, and Mirela's Bulgarian pastries are his favorite.

"I expect there's some. See what's in that cooler, will you?"

He opened a bottle of wedding-gift rosé for me and a bottle of apple juice for himself while I put out crackers and cheese. I wasn't used to just *being*, relaxing, with no phones ringing in the background and no querulous visitors with questions and complaints. We sat and said nothing for a moment, just looking at the ocean. I stretched out my legs. "I could get used to this."

He let that go for a moment before responding, my remark hanging in the air, totally out of character for me. "You *must* be relaxed," he observed. "You haven't mentioned the dead body for hours. Not like you, Detective Riley."

I made a face. Okay, so I had just been about to mention the dead body. "I met someone," I said instead. "A guy who lives in one of the other shacks, and feeds swallows. He called this Louis's shack."

Ali was still watching the ocean, stretching out to the horizon, and a whale-watch boat chugging along a couple of miles offshore. "So I heard."

"You heard? From whom?"

"Fellow down the beach."

I arched an eyebrow. "Was *he* catching anything?"

He cleared his throat. "Irrelevant," he said, which told me the other guy had indeed caught something. "Do you want to hear this or not?"

"Ooooh, irritated already? Of course I do. Go on."

"Well, I'd think you'd be interested. I'll bet this is the only dune shack with a curse."

I'd been about to take a sip of wine and now I spluttered it out again. "A curse? You're kidding! What kind of curse?"

"Well," he said, looking pleased, "how does a double murder-suicide work for you?"

Startled, I said, "When? Where? Here? Recently?"

"No, no, ages ago. During World War Two."

I put my glass down on the deck next to me and leaned forward. "So tell me."

He was still watching the whale boat. "So back in 1942 or sometime around then, this teenager got sent to live here, in this shack, to keep her safe from some potential bombing of Boston. Well, it wasn't bombed, of course, but no one really knew that, no one knew what was going to happen next. The family sent their German-born housekeeper along to take care of her."

"What was her name? The girl?"

He shrugged. "He didn't say."

I guessed it was significant that the housekeeper was German. "So what happened?"

"There was something about the housekeeper… oh, yeah, right. The U-boats."

"The U-boats?"

"German submarines."

I sighed. "I know what U-boats are. Or were. What about them?"

I had a sneaking feeling Ali was enjoying this. "They were patrolling the coastline, and—"

"Wait, what?" I held up a hand. "*This* coastline? This far from Europe? You're kidding." I associated World War Two with Europe and Japan, which just goes to show how little I learned about it in school.

"Not at all. Apparently the submarines were all up and down the East Coast, and they sent spies ashore. Saboteurs, too: he said a whole bunch got arrested in New York or New Jersey, someplace around there. They came in on Zodiacs, or the World War Two equivalent of Zodiacs, or if they were close enough, they just put on wetsuits and came swimming in." He caught my expression. "No, Sydney, I'm not making this up. I'm pretty sure I've already heard about it before, now that I think of it. Provincetown had a massive naval presence during the war. And it only makes sense they'd send people ashore—no one could find the U-boats, anyway. Definition of sneak attack. Here, on Cape Cod. In fact *right* here, on the backshore. That's how these people met up."

"You mean, this girl, and the German— oh, yeah, I think I see where this is going."

He nodded. "Fellow wasn't clear about the details, but there was also some girl from P'town involved, too, along with this German who came ashore." He sighed. "Like I said, he didn't know much about the specifics. He was more interested in the history—the submarines, and all the sailors in town, all that. He said you could walk across Provincetown Harbor stepping from Navy ship to Navy ship. So he didn't have a lot of real interest in what was supposed to be happening here, except he said two people were killed, one of them a suicide—no, don't look at me like that, I don't know who did what, but the result was the shack ended up being cursed. And the same family still has the lease on it, though we all know what *that* means at the moment."

I ignored the current political ramifications. "Has anyone else died? I mean, sustained the curse?"

"No, you bloodthirsty girl, he didn't say anyone since then *died*. But strange things happen here. Lights on inside at night when no one's in residence. Once a fishing boat was offshore and could swear the shack was on fire, but when the rangers came to investigate, there was nothing. Stuff like that."

"Ghost stories," I said.

He nodded. "People love them."

That's for sure. P'town's resident ghost hunter, Adam Berry, always gets quite a crowd at his annual Halloween exploration and there have been creepy cemetery tours for ages. There's even a book out, *Paranormal Provincetown*, though I've never read it.

Probably would now, though.

I picked up my wine again. "You think anything will happen while we're here?"

"I certainly hope not. This is supposed to be a honeymoon." He smiled. "I knew I should have held out for Paris instead."

"Paris will always be there," I said automatically. When Mike offered us the use of the dune shack as a wedding present I'd certainly jumped at the opportunity. It was unclear how much longer there would be an annual lottery for shack residencies. The leases granted by the National Seashore were ending, and the Seashore was renting them to the highest bidders. This, I knew, could be our last opportunity.

The shack being haunted? That was a bonus.

3

The dead lawyer didn't stay dead for long. At least not in my consciousness.

"I wonder how the investigation is going," I remarked to Ali on our third evening at the dune shack. We were eating dinner inside— the sheer number of bugs that congregated after sunset made any outside activities impossible; we slathered on insect repellent and made mad dashes to the outhouse when necessary—and you really had to admit that Adrienne the diva chef's idea of a picnic was better than most fine dining.

Reheated, of course. Okay, maybe not such fine dining.

We had a Coleman lantern in the corner, but candles on the table. Forewarned about the fact that the oil lamps supplied for us in fact offered precious little real light, we'd found a camping store online and provisioned ourselves. I had no idea whether we'd ever use any of it again, but you only go on your honeymoon once.

Well, in my case, once per marriage, anyway.

Ali filled my glass with Châteauneuf-du-Pape; in the candlelight it looked like liquid rubies. "I wondered when you'd bring that up again."

"Am I that predictable?"

He looked amused. "Only when it comes to murder," he said.

"Fair point," I conceded. "But I still wonder. Do you think it was a suicide?" I was savoring the taste of the wine on my tongue, rich and smooth, berries and candlelight and warmth.

"Having no information about it, I wouldn't leap to any conclusions," he said. "How does she make chicken taste this delicious?"

"Well, you don't have to leap, exactly. But you're in law enforcement, you know stuff—maybe take a few baby steps toward a conclusion?"

He sighed. He might be technically in law enforcement, but the only thing he investigates for Immigration & Customs Enforcement—a division of Homeland Security I generally despise, with the exception of Ali's department—is human trafficking. That meant he knew how to handle weapons (and once or twice in our relationship I'd had reason to be grateful for that), solve crimes, go undercover… but his work didn't put him inside the minds of other officers investigating completely different crimes.

Still, I always tried it. One of these days he might surprise me.

Pigs might be seen winging their way across the sky, too.

"Listen," said Ali. "It wasn't exactly the way we'd planned for the wedding to end, but no matter why he fell—yes, or jumped, or was pushed—it wasn't exactly *his* best day, either. Hopefully they've made some progress in figuring out what happened, so his family can have some peace around it."

I regarded him over the rim of my glass. "Ha. So you are admitting he *could* have been pushed."

"If the district attorney is investigating, yeah, that's a real option. But not the only one, *cara*. And none of our business."

I sighed. "I know," I said, sipped the wine, put the glass down, and took a bite of Adrienne the diva chef's idea of picnic food.

The chicken really was quite delicious. And Ali was probably right. But you don't have a dead man crash your wedding every day, either, and that made it—to my mind, anyway—a reasonable thing to want to discuss.

The problem being that I didn't have any information on how the investigation was progressing. Which, given my history and propensity for being around when dead bodies turn up, was a little frustrating. "I'd probably have it figured out by now," I said facetiously to Ali.

"Of course you would, *cara.*"

I paused for a beat. "It's a pity we can't find out."

He looked at me suspiciously. There were certain places in the dunes where cell phones could pick up a signal. We'd agreed not to try and find them—both Mike and Ali's supervisor knew how to reach us in case of an emergency—so that we could focus, after all the craziness of the last year or so, on just being together and enjoying ourselves. "It's a pity," he agreed cautiously. "But I'm reasonably sure you'll find out when we get home."

Home was, now, the penthouse apartment at the Race Point Inn, gifted to us by its former owner, Glenn, who now lived most of the year in Amsterdam. Home was where my cat, Ibsen, was probably being spoiled to pieces by various and sundry employees who'd volunteered to look after him in our absence. Home was, pretty much, where a lawyer called Barclay Cargill fell to his death. "Hang on, he couldn't have gotten into the *apartment*, could he?" I asked suddenly as the thought occurred. I hadn't tried to work out which window had given him access to the terrace where the wedding had been unfolding before it was interrupted.

It would feel very unsettling indeed to have either a murder or a suicide launched from our personal home.

"It wasn't a crime scene," Ali reminded me. "Julie said it was the third floor. Not that far to fall, really."

Two floors down from us. That was something of a comfort, anyway. "Julie talked to you about it? With me not there?"

"I do occasionally have conversations that don't involve you, *cara*."

"Yeah, yeah, I know…" I ate for a moment in silence, then swallowed and looked up. "They'll have gotten it figured out by the time we get back, anyway," I said.

"That's what I was saying."

"Because," I said, "if it's not solved in the first forty-eight hours, it's not usually solved, right?"

"You've been watching too many YouTube videos," he said. "You know as well as anybody that's not always the case. Often isn't, in fact." He finished the last of his green beans. "Anyway," he said, folding his napkin and putting it on the table, "you have another mystery to solve, don't you?"

"Do I?"

He smiled. He looked incredibly beautiful in the candlelight. "What happened to make our shack the nexus of a curse," he said.

There was that. "Okay," I said. "You're on. I'll find out about the ghost. In the meantime, what will you be doing?"

"As little as possible," said Ali.

***

Although I've sometimes been called Provincetown's answer to Miss Marple, secretly I'm more of a Nancy Drew girl. And it was with that in mind that I launched myself into *Sydney Riley and the Curse of the Dune Shack* the next day.

The first part, of course, was to explore the environment itself. I wished I'd bothered to seek out a map, if such a thing existed, but there was the wedding and all that… But now it was time to see what this alternate universe of sand and sea and sky was really about.

Our shack—"Louis's shack"—was a stone's throw away from the dune cliff, surrounded by sand and with the ever-changing vista of the sea stretching out to the horizon. I loved that closeness: Ali and I went to sleep and woke up to the sound of the waves lapping on the shore, and I wasn't missing the craziness of Commercial Street in the summer. The sounds wafting up to our apartment, especially in season, were quite different: loud voices, horns blaring, motorcycles roaring, cyclists with boom boxes… we had it all. The silence out here, by contrast, was just the tiniest bit jarring.

The shack itself comprised only one room, built—as far as I could see—of debris: pieces of wood bleached and smoothed by salt water, timbers so massive they could have only come from a shipwreck; plywood patches here and there. There were two big windows facing the water, where a door led out to the equally ramshackle porch; smaller windows in back, facing the sand and the mosses and the odd crippled trees stubbornly surviving in this windswept place.

Then there was the question of water. Down the hill, over a small rise, bucket in hand. Prime the pump. Pump the water, fill the bucket. Back up the rise, up the hill, the water sloshing all over. And, remember, these aren't just any hills: they are sand dunes. For every step you take, you slide back at least half a step, and usually more. You have to attack the sand with your toes, forcing them to find a grip, to hold it and your weight as your other foot does the same thing.

My first day out here, I'd spilled all the water before I made it to the top of the first rise.

Now I decided to risk rejection and pay another visit to the only person besides Ali I'd seen out here. The sounds of the surf on the sandbar and the beach faded behind me as I climbed; in minutes there was a high dune between me and the ocean, and I could be miles away from it, anywhere, in the desert or on the moon.

A hawk glided above me, intent on finding its breakfast. I was irrelevant to it; it was focused, intense, prepared for the sudden drop to earth allowing it to eat and live another day, the steep dive that brings death to one creature and life to another.

Birds were everywhere; the shorebird migration that takes them from the Arctic to South America had, extraordinarily, begun already, and terns were gathering on the sand, over the ocean, in the dunes, stocking up. I'd seen them in the evenings massing on the beach, thousands of them, and the jaegers harassing them for the fish they'd just caught. There are ospreys, too, hunting small mammals along the high-tide line to supplement their diet of fish, eating the meadow voles they find there.

It has to be said that I'm not a great Outdoor Girl; I've never been very interested before in nature as a concept, as an abstract. Oh, I'm happy enough to go out to Beech Forest and walk around the ponds there; I often drive out to Herring Cove to watch the sunset, or up to the Visitors' Center to wander some of the paths behind the outdoor amphitheater; I've even been known to walk on the beach on the harbor, across Commercial Street from the Race Point Inn. But spending time out here? There had been part of me that wanted to ask Mike if he was out of his mind, offering us this stay as a wedding present. Once upon a time, I'd moved to Provincetown from Cambridge. I'm far better at ordering takeout than I am at foraging for anything.

Still, even I had to admit, sun-bleached and weathered and barren as the dunes seem to be, there's something eloquent out here I hadn't really experienced before. (There are more things in heaven and earth, Riley, than are dreamt of…) It was starting to occur to me that I'd been missing out on something important, something essential in a way I hadn't really experienced before.

I retraced my steps to where I thought I remembered the old man with the swallow houses lived, only to find myself totally turned around. The sound of the ocean oriented me, and I stopped and listened for the waves. Literally retracing your steps didn't work out here: the sand made everything temporary, passages wiped away by the wind almost as soon as they appeared. In the mornings we found traces of the denizens of the night: coyote footprints, tiny crevasses created by the toads that apparently surrounded us after dark—a whole layer of life that went on unbeknownst to us.

I often think about layers when I'm walking in town. The layers of time, of course; we're all aware of those, of knowing that a hundred years before, someone else walked these streets, lived entire lives lost to us now, but lives that were as important to them as mine is to me. I once heard empathy defined that way—understanding that others' lives are as real to them as yours is to you.

But the layers don't stop there, do they? Because even in the same moment, different things are visible to different people. I walk down Commercial Street and I see the balloon man hanging out in front of town hall, and the buskers, and whoever is encouraging tourists to come and eat in their restaurants. I pass the trolley and wave to my friend Pat, the driver. I may stop in at Perfect Picnic to grab a baguettini for lunch; at Perry's for a bottle of Côtes du Rhône, at Hennep for some edibles to help me sleep. I'll see certain people I know and focus on them, excluding everyone else from my consciousness, unless they're doing something really remarkable.

Which actually isn't all that uncommon here.

But Mirela sees completely different things when she walks down Commercial. She has an eye on every single gallery along the way, checking out what other artists in town are doing; she likes the outdoor bar at the Crown & Anchor so usually checks in there; she loves the buskers and is great friends with Damian in particular, always keeping an eye out for him and stopping to listen; and throughout it all she's always noticing how people dress, because she likes to change her look.

And that's just someone whose life isn't dramatically different from mine. When a trans person walks down Commercial Street, they're seeing completely different people, noticing completely different things. Or a gay man who's into leather. Or a schoolteacher visiting for the first time. Or a marine biologist working at the Center for Coastal Studies. Or… or… or…

The point is, every place has layers, and some of those layers are mysterious, almost invisible, possibly even forbidden to those who don't have the key to their presence.

As I experienced a brief moment of—okay, it has to be said, panic—at not knowing precisely where I was in the dunes, I realized there are layers out here, too, only they're even more transient than the ones in town. In town, you can look at a building and remember what it used to be a couple of years or owners back; in the dunes, layers are erased almost as soon as they appear and are experienced.

I might never have found my way to the other shack, truth be told, if I hadn't heard voices. The air was still, as it tended to get in the hot afternoons, and sounds carried. I headed in the direction they seemed to be coming from, hoping it wasn't intrepid hikers who might be just as lost as I was.

It wasn't. I climbed another rise in the sand and suddenly found I had somehow accidentally stumbled exactly where I wanted to be: the shack in the depression, surrounded by birdhouses. The old man was standing in front of it, talking to a woman in the green-and-brown uniform of a park ranger.

She was the first to catch sight of me; people in law enforcement generally are. That has to be one of the first police academy classes—or, at the very least, mantras: notice everything. When we're out together, there isn't much that Ali misses; his cursory first glance is more penetrating than my fifth one will ever be, even when I'm concentrating.

She stopped mid-phrase and lifted an eyebrow, and I immediately felt awkward. "I'm—I'm sorry," I stammered. I didn't mean to interrupt."

"Are you lost?"

Not now I wasn't. I glanced from the ranger to the old man. "No, actually, I was here the other day, and I came back to—um, well, honestly, to hear more about the shack where I'm staying."

The old man said to the ranger, "She's at Louis's place. Name's Sydney Riley. Lives in town." He coughed on the last word; it had probably been a fairly long bit of dialogue from someone who lived alone out here.

The ranger smiled at me. "I'll bet Cyril gave you his version of a ghost story about some old curse on the shack," she said, and stretched out her hand. "Ranger Lucy O'Connell," she said. Her grip on my hand was firm.

"Sydney Riley," I responded automatically. "Oh, sorry—you already knew that."

The smile broadened. "Not much happens out here that Cyril Stephenson doesn't know about."

"Everyone knows about the curse," he said. He sat down on the rocking chair perched a trifle precariously on his rickety front deck, pulled out a pipe and tobacco tin, and started the smoking process by tamping tobacco into the pipe. I knew this was bound to take a while; my father had smoked a pipe until my mother's ranting about cancer made him finally and reluctantly give it up. But I remembered the comfort he took in the ritual, and the rich smell that for so many years had been a part of him. "Everyone knows. It ain't news no more."

"Everyone *you* talk to, anyway," said the woman.

"Have you seen anything—um, weird—out here, Ranger?" I asked.

She was still smiling. "Lucy," she corrected me.

"She's more informal than most of 'em," said Cyril to me.

"You're the one who started it," she told him.

"Damn right. Not going to call a girl half my age Ranger," he grunted, and applied himself to the pipe.

The light danced in her eyes. "More like a third your age." This was clearly a conversation with which they were both familiar.

"So is it just a story?" I asked her. I was almost holding my breath; I was going to be very disappointed if she said yes.

She moved into the shade of the shack—the sun was in fact getting a little too warm for comfort, and there were few enough places out here to find shade—and perched on the edge of the deck. It looked like it might come down at any moment. "Depends on who you ask," she said. "The park superintendent would tell you it's an old wives' tale."

"Old wives know a lot," said Cyril. He was on his third or fourth try to light the pipe.

Experience with my father told me this might be the one to work.

"You'd think, actually, that more of the shacks would be haunted," Lucy said slowly, as though the thought had just occurred to her. "Once upon a time, there was a lot of death out here. Bodies were washing up all the time from shipwrecks, and even survivors didn't always make it. But you never hear stories about any of the other shacks."

There was a moment of silence. Around us, the swallows swooped into the birdhouses and then sped away. I thought about the nests inside, with hungry mouths to feed.

Cyril removed the pipe from his mouth. "Ghosts have better sense than to come out here," he observed. "Nobody to notice them."

"There's you," Lucy offered.

He shook his head and puffed on the pipe. He seemed to have it under control at last.

I could feel sweat trickling down my neck and under my armpits. "Can I—would you mind if I sat down?" There wasn't another chair, but if the deck could take Lucy's weight then I was probably okay as well. And the shade would be glorious.

She moved over and patted the wooden planks next to her. "Come on. You really should wear a hat if you're out walking and," looking at me more critically, "carry a water bottle. You can get in trouble out here pretty quickly."

"Sorry." I wedged myself onto the deck so I could see both of them. "So, my shack—"

"Louis's shack," said Cyril.

"Someone died there," Lucy said. "Back during World War Two. No one really knows the details. Long before our time." I resisted looking at Cyril; he could be any age, but it wasn't *impossible* that he'd been alive then. "Some retired professor was in town back in the 1990s, and she talked to some of the rangers then. She said she'd stayed at the shack during the war, but no one paid much attention. She was related to Louis, wasn't she, Cyril?"

"Happen so," he said, nodding.

"Not sure how, though." She shrugged and turned back to me. "But you see, that's the perfect basis for a ghost story," she said. "Just enough content to sound a little creepy. And then whoever tells the story can add in their own details."

I was fascinated. I'd been out with my friend Rob who owns Art's Dune Tours, and they *never* talked about ghosts or curses, despite seemingly knowing everything there was to know about the dunes. "So which is it?" I asked. "A ghost, or a curse?"

Cyril removed the pipe from his mouth. "Happen you can have both."

"If there's a curse, no one knows exactly what it's about," said Lucy. "Like, who specifically is cursed, and what the curse entails. Which are kind of essential elements to a curse, wouldn't you say?" She laughed. "To the best of my knowledge, no one who's stayed there has ever been hurt, and isn't that what curses are mostly about?"

"Maybe it's the building, not the people," I said.

Lucy looked amused. "Watch yourself," she advised. "You're veering into political waters. Not a good idea. These days, the whole service thinks all the shacks are cursed."

"Doomed, you mean," said Cyril.

She shot him a look. "No politics," she said.

"Just sayin' what I'm seein'."

"So," I said, dragging the conversation back onto relatively safer ground, not that much unlike the old guardians pulling a man from a sinking ship, "you don't have anything more specific? I'm disappointed—I wanted a good juicy ghost story. I was hoping to scare my boyfri—my husband." Oops. Wasn't quite used to that one yet.

Cyril said, "Happen I seen lights there."

Lucy looked up at him. The sun had shifted slightly, and she had to shade her eyes "*Have* you?" she asked. "I didn't know that. When?"

"When shack's boarded up," he said.

"Did you check it out?"

He shrugged and tapped his pipe on the edge of his chair to remove the ash. "Happen none of my business," he said.

She shook her head. "Cyril, who knows what you see out here when the shacks are boarded up?" she said. She slid off the deck onto the sand and dusted off her pants, picking up her hat and putting it back on her head. "I'm off," she announced. "Sydney? Want me to show you the way back?"

I was bemused. "Is it that obvious? That I'm lost, I mean?"

"It's dangerous to walk around unprotected," she said, shrugging. So obviously it *was* obvious. "Wear a hat and carry some water. And if you take off those sneakers, wear socks: the sand'll burn your feet. Come on, I'll walk with you."

I jumped down to join her. "Nice to talk with you," I said to Cyril.

"Always here," he said.

Lucy tipped her hat in his direction. "Be seeing you."

He waved her off. "Not too soon."

She laughed and led me away from his shack. "Cyril's a character," she said.

"Where does he go in the winter?" I asked. I knew that currently all the shacks were boarded up once the gales and nor'easters started in earnest. "The swallows all leave, don't they?"

"He has a room in town," she said. "Spends most of his time at the Old Colony Tap." She glanced at me, a quick, birdlike gesture. "Keeps himself to himself. Still hikes out every week or so to check on the place."

"What did you think of his story?" I asked. "Did he really see lights?"

"What you didn't see," she said crisply, "is the mountain of bottles behind his shack; he pays someone to haul 'em out for him. Anything he thinks he saw, he wasn't alone. Jack Daniel's was sure to be there, too."

"Oh, like that," I acknowledged. I found myself oddly deflated.

Lucy laughed. "Don't be discouraged," she said. "Maybe you'll meet up with a ghost while you're there."

"That, or get cursed," I said.

She smiled. "There's that," she said. "Let's go this way; it's more scenic." She led me past a small copse of stunted trees and up a rise and then there we were, suddenly it seemed, on the high dune cliff above the beach, with the ocean stretching out sparkling in the sunlight, a fishing boat with its outriggers lifted, steaming back toward Provincetown. Picture-postcard-perfect. "There we are," said Lucy. She was looking out at the horizon.

"It's beautiful," I said, though I wasn't a hundred percent sure. There's something about a stretch of anything, be it sand or ocean, that's flat—it's hard to take in. There isn't anything to frame the view, to give it perspective. No points of reference.

Except the one lonely fishing boat.

Lucy's mind was elsewhere. "It's why I love my job," she said softly. "Come on, this way."

We walked for a few moments in silence. "What do *you* do, in the winter?" I asked.

She looked amused. "Oh, I'm still here. I'm not one of the seasonal rangers," she said. "We still keep an eye on things out in the Province Lands, even in the off-season. Hikers still come out; boats still get marooned. Things like that. I think I love it even more in the winter."

Better you than me, I thought. It got wild enough in town, sometimes, when the winds came up and the tides surged; I couldn't imagine it in this desolate moonscape. "Did you grow up on the Cape?"

She shook her head, her eyes on the cliff path. "Maybe that's why I love it so much. I grew up in Dorchester. Um, that's part of Boston—"

"I know," I said. "I know Dorchester. I used to live in Cambridge."

"Then you can imagine it," she said, nodding.

I wasn't sure I could. "What was it like?"

She took a breath and looked at the path, not at me. "Three-decker houses and everyone in and out of each other's kitchens. The smell of cabbage and gossip. And poverty—they try not to let it show. All us Irish families in the neighborhood, we didn't starve, it wasn't that kind of poverty. We had something slightly more genteel: blue-collar poverty. Hand-me-down clothes and sharing a room with your three sisters. Our fathers, they were all firefighters or police officers or construction workers. We ate, yeah, but it wasn't enough to sustain dreams on."

"But you went into law enforcement," I pointed out, and she laughed.

"Yeah, I guess you could say that. Take the girl out of Dorchester, never take Dorchester out of the girl."

"And Cyril? Where did he come from?"

She stopped so abruptly I bumped into her. "You know, it hasn't come up," she said, sounding surprised. "Cyril doesn't talk much, and never about himself. You were lucky he put up with us that long. He must have taken a shine to you."

"Really? He disguised it well."

She laughed and set off again. "That's Cyril. Laconic doesn't even begin to describe him. I've known him over five years and don't really know that much about him. Like I said, he likes to keep himself to himself."

We walked on in silence, though in my case trudging would be the more accurate description. She was right about the sun and the dehydration. "There," she said finally. "Your shack is that way—just follow this path through the dune grasses."

"Oh! I just realized… you must be the ranger we've seen a couple of times walking along the dune cliff there." *Detective Riley at your service: the first to notice the obvious.*

She smiled. "It was good meeting you, Sydney."

"You, too," I said automatically. "And… thanks."

"Make sure you wear that hat," she said. "And your husband, too. His skin might be darker than yours, but he'll burn, too." And she continued along the cliff path, leaving me staring after her.

And wondering how she knew that Ali was Lebanese.

4

The sun came in at its usual straight-into-your-eyes five-o'clock-in-the-morning angle. I stirred, reaching over beside me. No Ali.

I managed to get myself out of bed and stumbled, blinking, onto the deck. Instead of finding my husband sipping coffee and looking at the ocean, I found him in hiking boots and khaki shorts. He'd clearly already been down to pump water and was pouring some into a couple of bottles. "What are you doing up?" I asked, half of it coming through a yawn. I don't care what anybody says, this is no hour to be up and about.

"Getting ready," said Ali.

"For what?" Then I really took in his full outfit of shorts and shirt and those damned boots. "What are you doing?" I repeated. He looked suspiciously energetic.

"We agreed we were hiking out to Race Point today," he said.

"I never agreed to hike to Race Point," I said automatically. And then I remembered last night's empty bottle of wine and … well, the rest of the night. "Did I really say that?"

"You did," he confirmed. Far too cheerful.

I gestured. "You go," I said. "Wake me when you're home." I turned to go back inside, and he caught my wrist. "You agreed," he reminded me.

I scowled at him, at the water, at the sky. "And what do I get in return?"

"Thought you'd already got it," he said. Okay, point taken. But honestly, when you're marooned out in a shack in the middle of shifting sands and on the edge of an ocean, what else is there to suggest… besides sex?

Well, apparently, a hike to Race Point.

I sighed with careful exaggeration and took my wrist back. "Okay, okay," I said irritably. "You shouldn't have let me drink so much last night."

"You never would have agreed in the first place if I hadn't let you drink so much last night."

There was that. "Okay, okay. But I need coffee first." I always needed coffee first.

"Ten minutes," he said. "I'm getting more water."

I watched him go down the dune toward the pump with his two empty gallon containers. Part of me was still marveling that there was a potable water table under the shifting sands of the dunes.

Meanwhile, though, I wasn't altogether pleased with what was happening. Against all odds, Ali was turning into something of a Nature Boy. I was pretty sure I didn't like the transformation.

And that's why a half-hour later I found myself at water's edge, trudging northward. The sun was getting hot, but fortunately the microscopic bugs that live where the ocean meets the shore are less active during the day (as well any self-respecting bug—or human—should be), and the sand here was less arduous to walk on. I'd taken Lucy's cautions to heart and was wearing my Tilley hat and carrying enough water for a small army. Plus, I was finding a lot of pretty shells and pebbles I kept picking up. Within the first half-hour, my pockets were bulging.

Ali had fashioned himself a walking stick from some driftwood. I squinted at him. "You're not bringing that home, are you?"

"I won't if you won't."

"If I won't what?"

He gestured toward my shorts. "Fill the apartment with shells and sand," he said.

I tossed my head with as much dignity as I could muster. "I'll sort through them."

"Of course you will, *cara.*"

The walk continued. It's a long way around the outer bend of the Cape, and why anyone would want to walk to Race Point baffled me.

It's not named that for any kind of "race" that was ever held. (Though now that I mention it, there *was* the famous Lipton Cup race between the fishermen of Provincetown and those of Gloucester, which P'town's *Rose Dorothea* won even with a crippled spar, but the truth was I had no idea where that had been held. It was, after all, 1911.) Instead, the place where a bay and an ocean come together is called a race: the waters are churning and treacherous, and the commercial fishermen and the whale boats and even the fast ferry navigate it carefully. Race Point is at the race, and curving a bit more toward the bay—and Provincetown itself—is the Race Point Light Station, these days fully automated but once the domain of another careful guardian of the shore.

Now, of course, it's an historic marker, and is maintained by the American Lighthouse

Foundation, which also maintains the lighthouses closer in to P'town, Wood End and Long Point. Times have changed.

They even did away with all the foghorns because the sound was bothering the gentle sensibilities of the newest generation of washashores—the wealthy ones. Can't have quaint Cape Cod be too quaint, after all. These days, if you need to hear their guidance, you use your smartphone to activate them— there's a number to call.

Walking in the sand is like nothing else. It's as if every step dares you to take the next. "Oh, so you thought that was easy? Well, try this!" I live on Cape Cod; of course I'm used to walking on sand. For small distances. Preferably with a car nearby to take me somewhere else when I'm done. I've done plenty of walking on the bay side of Provincetown and Truro, even some walking along the shore at Herring Cove.

Walking from the dune shack to Race Point was nothing like that. The sun was hot; hell, the *sand* was hot (not surprisingly, they leave a welcome sheet at the dune shack that specifies you should wear socks if you go for walks in the dunes, and Lucy had reminded me of that yesterday). "I hope you know," I panted at one point, "that this isn't going to be a daily feature of our married life."

"I don't expect it to be an ever-again feature of our married life," said Ali calmly. "It's why I figured we'd do it now."

"You're not even breathing hard," I said suspiciously. Ali doesn't go to the gym.

That I know of.

"If we loop around," he said, ignoring me, "we can stop in and say hi to your friend with the swallows."

"Cyril," I said a little breathlessly. "Cyril—Stephenson, I think."

"That's the one," he confirmed. "Do you want to take a break?"

What I really wanted was to be sitting in the shade with a fan on me and something very cold to drink in my hand. "Sure," I said.

We sat and drank cold water from our insulated cups and I picked up a few more random shells. "You know I did a Tarot spread the morning of the wedding," I said.

"That sounds nice and Catholic to me," commented Ali.

I didn't answer that—he's right, after all, I suspect the Church's view of fortunetelling is pretty negative—but went on with my thought instead. "It was mostly auspicious," I said.

"Meaning what, exactly?" Ali might be a fairly nonpracticing Muslim, but that doesn't mean he's gone over to necromancy, either. Nor truly have I. My Tarot deck was a somewhat tongue-in-cheek gift from Barry, my first boss in Provincetown who'd died at the Race Point Inn, and I usually think of it as something of a party trick. "Meaning we'll probably have an exciting life together," I said.

He gave me a wry smile. "Tell me something I don't know," he said.

I leaned my head against his shoulder. "It's been pretty good so far, hasn't it? I don't mean marriage or anything like that—I mean us, you know. Together."

His arm came up around my shoulder. "Yes, *cara*," he said softly. "It's been pretty good so far."

Later, as we were walking back—because you can't ever just walk to someplace, you have to come back, too—a dark shape suddenly lifted itself out of the surf, another right behind it, and I gasped. "What the—Oh! It's seals!"

"What did you think it was?"

I shrugged. "I don't know. People. Frogmen. Something scary." We gave the seals a wide berth—people forget that what looks cute from a distance is actually a large carnivorous wild animal that likes its privacy—and then I added, "Maybe just because I was thinking about that story. You know, about the submarines here during the Second World War." We went a few more steps. "Which I still have trouble believing."

"Why?"

I shrugged. "It just seems so—I don't know, what's the word? Fantastic? Implausible? I mean, look." I pointed offshore, where a few small commercial fishing boats were chugging determinedly away. Off on the horizon, something bigger, a container ship probably, just on the edge of the world. "How far in would they have to come, to drop people off?"

Ali looked baffled. "I'm no mariner," he pointed out. "But there's no reason it couldn't work. Submarine could surface in the dark, offload the people—"

"—Frogmen?"

He sighed. "I don't think they're called that anymore, *cara*. But whomever, and then the sub just goes down again and they come onshore. Happens all the time."

Startled, I said. "Wait—you mean now?"

"I do." He looked, if anything, amused. "People who aren't supposed to be coming into the United States have used stranger methods. Not big military submarines, of course; but on submersibles from larger ships, for sure. It's expensive so it's not your run-of-the-mill human trafficking, but if someone wants to come in, it's not unknown."

"But not here, on Cape Cod?"

"Not to my knowledge."

I sighed and looked back at the water. The seals had disappeared. But I had a feeling I was going to see them again in those liminal moments between waking and sleeping, their dark figures emerging from the water, taking to the land as if they owned it.

***

Cyril wasn't all that pleased to see us. "Thought you'd left," he said to me. "Who's this?"

"My—um—husband," I said, trying out the unfamiliar word again. "Ali Hakim, this is Cyril—Stephenson? Is that it?"

Ali had the good sense to not offer his hand, and Cyril just leaned back in his chair, regarding us as though we too were aliens from the sea.

"We were passing," said Ali. "We don't mean to disturb you." He grabbed my elbow. "Nice meeting you," he added with some finality.

"Happen," said Cyril, "was going to have a smoke."

Not being entirely sure whether that meant settle in or get out, I cleared my throat. "We're leaving in another day," I said. "And—"

Cyril was looking at Ali. "Arab fellow?" he inquired.

"Second generation," Ali said pleasantly. "My parents are from Lebanon."

Cyril nodded, as though that told him something. "You can sit."

We perched on the rickety porch, which did everything but sigh at our combined weight—and neither of us is fat. I hoped it wouldn't collapse today. Around us, the swallows wheeled and dived. I cleared my throat and shook my empty water bottle. "Do you have water?" I asked, craning to look behind me, into his shack. "I've run out."

"Nope," he answered quickly, almost before I'd gotten the question out. "Have to go to the pump myself later." He was still looking at Ali. "Happen I know you?"

Ali shook his head, settling himself slightly more comfortably on the decking. "I don't believe so," he said. "Maybe you've seen me around? Where do you go in the winter? We live in Provincetown."

Cyril started filling his pipe. "Her," he said, jerking his head in my direction, "I know about. One of them fancy inns, she owns. That's her. Now I'm tryin' to place you." He applied the first match to the pipe, and I wondered how he knew I co-owned the Race Point Inn. Certainly I hadn't told him—or Lucy, for that matter.

Ali shrugged carelessly, but I could see something in his eyes, a quickening of interest. "Don't think we've met," he said.

Cyril tried another match, inhaled, still not getting the draw he was looking for. "Maybe not," he conceded once he could take a breath.

Since that conversation seemed to be spluttering as much as Cyril's pipe, I tried something fresh. "When do the swallows leave?" I asked, gesturing around to the birdhouses. There was a solitary birdhouse at the shack where we were staying, and there were still a lot of swallows in the air, snapping up all the bugs that tortured us; here, with so many birdhouses, it seemed the air was thick with the graceful swooping bodies. And while we were still in August, fall would come, and Cyril and swallows would all have to leave. The backshore is no place to winter over.

He finally had the pipe under control, and released a plume of smoke into the air.

"September migration," he said. It was unclear whether he meant the birds or himself. "Another month, they'll all be gone." He slanted us a look. "You'll be long gone, too," he added.

"Just back to town," said Ali. He sounded offhand, but I could sense he was intensely interested in the old man. I wondered why. "Like you?"

Another long puff. "Happen I stay there," Cyril acknowledged. I imagined him in his rented room, trekking down to the Old Colony to sit morosely at the bar, making do through the winter, waiting for the spring so he could take the boards down off his shack and take up residence again. I wondered what his situation was vis-à-vis the park service. There had been controversy when they'd begun terminating old leases on the shacks that remained after the wholesale destruction of the 1980s; he had to have some serious connections. Lucy? I couldn't imagine a mere ranger would have that kind of pull.

Still, it seemed bad form to ask. Instead I said, a little inanely, "You're welcome to come by the Race Point Inn anytime, if you'd like company, I mean. We're open all winter—the bars and restaurant. I know it can get lonely."

Good one, Riley: you're talking about loneliness to someone who's clearly chosen a solitary life.

Cyril ignored me. "Seen you up to the old police station," he said to Ali. "Happen I remember now."

"That's possible," said Ali. "I know some people there."

"Happen seen you more than once." Cyril was looking at the cloudless blue sky as though he'd tired of the conversation, but there was an edge to his voice.

I felt like I was watching a tennis match, their verbal sparring sailing over the net only to be returned smartly. "We're friends with the chief detective," I said. That was pushing things just a little—I'm not entirely sure Julie Agassi counted me as much a friend as I thought of her as one—but it *was* odd, how Cyril kept needling Ali.

Ali seemed in no need of my intervention. "I'm in law enforcement myself," he said, still watching Cyril. "I work for Homeland Security."

There was a faint reaction, perhaps, in a flicker of the eyes as they rested briefly on Ali and then looked away again, but nothing more; Cyril had already known.

I wondered why.

Cyril decided he'd had enough. He knocked the ash out of his pipe and revoltingly cleared his throat. "Can't say we don't need it," he said.

"Need what?"

"Security." He looked amused. "For the homeland."

Ali leaned back on his elbows. "Something you're trying to tell me?" he asked, and in contrast to his posture his voice had turned dangerous, the way it did when something was at stake.

Cyril shook his head. "Passin' the time," he said. "Happen you're the ones come to visit me. Not askin' anything I shouldn't." He shrugged. "Don't have no reason to. We're used to law enforcement out here. Rangers showin' up at all hours."

"You and Ranger O'Connell seem to be good friends," I said.

"Me an' Lucy got an understandin'," he said, nodding.

"And what's that?" asked Ali amiably.

"What d'you mean?"

"Your understanding with Ranger O'Connell," he said. "What is it?"

Cyril finally looked straight at him. "She don't bother me, I don't bother her," he said. "That kind of understanding. Knowing how to take each other." He paused. "Knowing when a conversation's over," he added pointedly.

Ali sat up, hopped off the deck, made a point of dusting off the seat of his jeans. "And so do we," he said. "Nice seeing you, sir." That "sir," I knew, was ominous; it's the stilted politeness of a law enforcement officer who might be about to make your day get very bad indeed. It was the same kind of courtesy that cops use when they pull you over.

Or when they're about to arrest you.

I couldn't understand what exactly had passed between these two that had made it necessary, but I was ready to be out of there. We could watch swallows at our shack, too. I slid off the deck and turned to Cyril. "Thanks for your time," I said, aware of how lame that sounded. I was not going to add "have a nice day."

I didn't have to. Ali did it for me.

On the way back along the high dune path, I asked him what that was about. "Were you seriously thinking there was something wrong?"

"Not necessarily," said Ali. "And if there was, it'd be none of our business."

"He didn't want me going in the cottage," I said uncertainly.

"Probably didn't want you to see what a mess it was," said Ali. We crested the last hill and saw "our" shack, Louis's shack, high up on the next ridge. "It's been a nice break," Ali said. "It feels like a different world. Maybe everything at home will feel dull and tame after this."

He couldn't have been more wrong if he'd tried.

5

Coming back to the Race Point Inn was something of an anticlimax.

We'd left the place in turmoil. Wedding guests, including our families, everywhere; a dead body being discussed and transported; and all that on top of the usual bustle of summer visitors. The visitors were still there when we got back, but the body—and, possibly even more importantly, my mother—were thankfully absent.

In fact, it felt for the first few moments as if we were ourselves the visitors, coming into the lobby with our suitcases; I even had my camera slung over my shoulder. Just another couple of tourists, us.

And then the illusion faded and I found myself looking around with a more professional eye. Ever since Mike and I had been gifted—there was no other word—with the inn's ownership, I'd had to pay more attention to the names of employees, especially the gaggle of ridiculously handsome young men who rotated endlessly through the Race Point as waitstaff, bartenders, pool attendants, housekeeping, and clerks. I used to think of them collectively as "the Kevins" back when I was the inn's wedding coordinator and didn't have any investment in getting to know them all; those days were over. I was pleased to recognize the Kevin behind the reception desk as someone named Grant.

Gorgeous, of course. I don't know where all these guys come from—Mike and Wendy, the inn's general manager, do all the hiring—but it's decent marketing in a town that's considered a gay resort destination. And to be fair, they're all more than competent.

The lobby was bustling, but in a healthy way. A couple was sitting on what was my father's favorite loveseat, their heads together, consulting an iPad. A woman with a large hat and even larger handbag, texting even as she walked through in the direction of one of the inn's bars (we have four of them, one attached to the restaurant, one a tiki bar outside by the pool, one a more casual tavern, one a polished-mahogany-and-ferns affair). Three young men checking in. Another couple coming down the staircase, chattering together about their plans for the evening.

All pretty normal.

I snagged the elevator before anyone else could, and we got our bags in and used our key for restricted access to the penthouse. I was almost afraid to open the door: we were either going to be greeting with wild affection or treated to a very cold shoulder indeed from our feline housemate, Ibsen. I had a feeling it was going to be the latter. I've known this cat for many years and lost any illusions I'd ever had about him a long time ago.

The elevator door purred open, which was more than I could say for Ibsen. He stood in the foyer, fur bristling, tail waving and, I could swear, murder in his eyes. Ali held the door for me and we both lugged suitcases and tote bags in. Ibsen hissed, turned, and ran away.

"Just a trifle dramatic," commented Ali.

"You can say that again."

"Hmm." The elevator doors shut behind us, and I collapsed on the Regency sofa the penthouse's previous occupant, Glenn, had placed under the Charles Hawthorne painting that had once been at the center of a fraud investigation. When Glenn had given us the penthouse apartment, we'd been living in a postage-stamp-sized place above a nightclub, the only really notable piece of furniture being a sofa that routinely did a Little Shop of Horrors act and threatened to consume whomever was sitting there. We hadn't brought any of it with us. Glenn's taste in décor was good, if not precisely the same as mine, and once he'd moved all his personal items out, Ali and I decided to take redecorating the place slowly.

As in, to date, not at all.

"I," said Ali, "am taking a shower. A long, hot shower." We'd had an outdoor solar-operated almost-shower at the shack, but somehow with the struggle to pump water and bring it up the dune and pour it into the plastic and wait for it to heat up… well, that hadn't happened with any regularity. Not everyone's idea of a honeymoon, but there we were.

"Go for it," I said, kicking off my sandals. "I don't think I'm moving for the next three days."

"I was going to suggest you might want to join me."

I flapped a hand in his direction. "Romeo, I wouldn't even have the beaurgy."

"Your loss." He grinned suddenly, vividly, and I felt a wave of something all over again. Love? Lust? I was too tired to tell.

He hadn't been gone three minutes before the buzzer sounded. I managed to lift myself and stumble across to the intercom beside the elevator. "Irritable tourism central," I said. "Irritable tourist speaking."

There was a chuckle on the other end. "Jamie told me you were back," said Mike.

"Who's Jamie?"

"New events coordinator," he said. "Kathryn quit after—"

"After my wedding," I said wearily. I'd had a feeling. She'd been looking very green around the gills the last time I'd seen her, which was standing over a crushed body on the terrace. Not everybody's cup of tea. "Is she working out?"

"Who?"

"This Jamie," I said impatiently.

"Jamie's a he, and have a heart, he only started yesterday. I thought it was pretty amazing getting someone on board this fast. Wendy found him. He used to do weddings in Chatham."

Chatham: big wedding destination for big weddings. "Okay," I said cautiously. "How did he know I'm back?"

"Because he's good at his job," said Mike. "You sound cranky, Sydney. Is everything okay?"

"Of course it is," I said, instantly contrite. "Just tired. It was a wonderful gift, Mike, this week out there. Thank you again."

"Pleasure. Glad you enjoyed it. You coming down later?"

"Possibly," I said cautiously. What I'd been thinking of was a glass of wine and a pizza, not work, but maybe… "What have you found out?" I demanded.

"About what?"

"Don't play innocent," I said. "The body. The person. The victim. The guy who interrupted my wedding."

"Oh, *that*," Mike said carelessly. "Might have something, but if you're too tired…"

"I'll be down in half an hour."

I went and started yanking clothes out of the closet. Ali came into the bedroom, absently drying his hair with a towel. "You're looking very energetic there, *cara*."

"I have to go downstairs," I said, finally finding the skirt I was looking for. I held up a shirt. "Do these go together?"

"Since when have you asked my advice on fashion?" He sat down on the edge of the bed. "Not that it's a bad idea, mind you. I do have, if I say so myself, a certain sartorial panache…"

"They'll have to do." I was in and out of the shower in record time, pulling the shirt over my head. "I'm going to go talk to Mike."

Ali was dressed and looked a lot fresher than I felt. He was already putting the contents of our luggage into the washing machine. "I figured as much," he said.

I stopped. "You're doing laundry."

"Nothing escapes you, does it?" he asked admiringly. "You must be a detective or something."

I made a face. After all, *he* was the real detective in the family. Now that we were a family. "I won't be long."

"He knows something about your dead body, doesn't he?" He straightened up, my bathing suit still in his hand, and his eyes widened. "He does, doesn't he?"

"It's not my dead body."

"No," he agreed with something of a disarming twinkle. "I can vouch for your body being alive and well and—"

"Shh." I kissed him. "Be back soon."

When Glenn moved to Amsterdam and Mike and I assumed co-ownership of the inn, I'd moved from the small cupboard out of which I'd worked as events coordinator into Glenn's former office, across a small entryway from Mike's. Ali and I hadn't done much to change the penthouse, but I went a little wild with my new professional space, luxuriating in the big room. Soft colors, a feature wall of Provincetown photography, lilac and white accents, a real rug, fresh flowers. A statement office, I suppose.

I didn't even bother going in. Mike's door was open and I flopped into one of his client chairs. "So tell me."

"Nice to see you, too, Sydney," he said, looking up from his laptop, his blue eyes amused.

"Okay," I said, and ticked a few items off on my fingers. "The dunes were great, thank you again for sending us out there, we walked all the way to Race Point, which I will never ever do again in my whole life, the shack you put us in is apparently cursed, and I'm in love with my husband." There: I'd said it right the first time, that odd new word in my vocabulary. "Good enough?"

He laughed at that. "Good enough," he agreed, and shut the laptop, leaning back in his well-padded leather executive chair, clasping his hands behind his neck. "Okay. So. Mirela knows more than I do, but—"

"Wait," I interrupted. "*Mirela* knows more than you do? How does that work? She's an artist."

"She's an artist who is dating one of the Barnstable County assistant district attorneys," he said. "You want details on her love life, you'll have to talk to her."

"Fair enough." I made a mental note. "Proceed."

"Well, Mr. Barclay Cargill checked in here three days before your wedding. He'd made the reservation—or someone made it on his behalf—a month ago. Online. His briefcase— which Wendy says he had with him at check-in—wasn't anywhere, so the supposition is that whoever sent him out that window took it with them. There wasn't much of interest in his suitcase, but he didn't have any of the usual stuff—shorts, t-shirts, swim trunks, anything you'd take on vacation."

"So he was here on business," I said, nodding.

"That's what the police think. Or what Mirela says the DA says."

"What kind of business?" I asked. The suit was a red flag; very few people in P'town wear suits, and certainly not in the late-August heat. There aren't any corporate offices here—a couple of real estate and estate planning attorneys, sure, but even they tended toward chinos and sport shirts. I couldn't think of anywhere you'd go where you'd need to wear a business suit. Well—red flag or red herring. Who knew?

"No idea," said Mike.

"And it couldn't have been an accident?" Not if the DA and the state police were involved a week on, I thought. "Or a suicide?"

Mike shook his head. "He was thrown," he said. "So sayeth the coroner, apparently."

"You spoke to the coroner?"

"Via Mirela," he clarified.

"And it's definitely not suicide?" Now that I'd had time to think about it, I knew it wouldn't have been an accident; the windows didn't open wide enough for it to make sense to stumble out, no matter how drunk the person.

Mike grunted. "Unless he managed to leap up *and* backward through the window."

"You know a lot about it," I commented.

"I know Mirela," said Mike.

"He was a lawyer, right?" I asked. "What about that? What kind of law? Did he have enemies?" I was thinking maybe criminal law and Mafioso types running amuck. Okay, so I needed to get some sleep.

He lowered his arms and leaned forward again in the chair. "Don't know about enemies," he said. "But I know what he did. What kind of law her practiced, I mean."

"Which was?"

He was watching me for my reaction. "Property development and land use," he said.

"Whew." I thought about it for a moment. "Talk about a hot-button issue."

It was probably the most vital—and controversial—conversation happening on Cape Cod. Not necessarily new, but incredibly intense. We weren't alone—many other coastal communities in the world have been gradually experiencing what in the city would be called gentrification: old buildings purchased and then demolished to make way for new ones that soaked up none of the character and essence of the old ones, so that eventually every "unique" locale was going to look and feel and function like every other one. Wealthy people moving in and pushing up real estate prices—along with prices for everything else—so that townies were forced to leave. A sign in one of the Outer Cape's town halls reads, "Wouldn't it be nice if the people who work in this building could afford to live in this town?"

Nantucket and Martha's Vineyard had already gone too far down that route to ever come back. I used to say, "unless a bad hurricane hits and wipes them out," but then someone, maybe Mirela, pointed me to Naomi

Klein's book about devastation capitalism, and I realized that even that wouldn't save anybody.

Along with a wave of corporations buying up some of the area's most iconic (and formerly individualistic and even eccentric) establishments, there had recently been another wave of development-development-development. I'd come to hate the word: they weren't really developing anything, they were building. On every possible *inch* of land. The only reason any of us could see the ocean at all was thanks to the National Seashore, Lucy's employer, which was keeping the public in public lands—but there were developers going right up to the edge and constantly pushing the boundaries. The image I had was of ravenous wolves slinking around the edge of a campfire, waiting for one unwary moment, waiting to grab what they wanted.

And attorneys were at the forefront of the wolfpack.

I met Mike's eyes. "Not any shortage of suspects, then," I said.

"Not the kind who generally resort to violence," he said mildly.

"Push anyone far enough, and… oops." Definitely too soon, but the gaffe had been unintentional.

"Not the best solution," he said. He was starting to shuffle papers around on the desk. There are people who work with pristine desktops; Mike is not one of them. "Always someone else in the queue to take their place."

"Lawyers being expendable?"

"You tell me." He shrugged. "Never heard of it stopping anything going forward, when there's money to be made."

I thought about it some more, nibbling at my bottom lip. Ali says I look like a rabbit when I do that. "Maybe it was personal," I said uncertainly.

"Always an option." He cleared his throat. "There's a widow; she was staying with him, and came back and collected his stuff once the police released the room. And the window's been repaired."

"Oh my gosh." I was coming slowly into understanding my responsibilities as co-owner. "Of course. Thanks for taking care of that." Not that I'd had a lot of time to take charge, what with the wedding and the honeymoon and all. "Is—um—anyone staying there now?" All we needed was a room with a reputation for defenestration of its occupants.

"We're full up," said Mike. "No one's giving up a reservation in August. And it's not like he died in the room."

I gave him a quick glance. "That's cold."

"That's reality."

"Okay." I stood up. "I'll get back to work tomorrow," I promised.

He waved a hand negligently. Mike has a bigger percentage of the inn ownership than I do, but he does the lion's share of the work, too, though I'm still not entirely sure exactly what it is he does. We do have a manager, after all. "Take your time. Everything's fine here. Adrienne, Martin, Wendy, everyone's doing their job. It's a well-oiled machine."

"Thanks to you."

"Thanks to Barry," he said seriously. Barry, the inn's original owner and my friend, Glenn's partner, a vibrant, kind man reduced to a dead body floating in the pool one morning. Come to think of it, no one was overly concerned about using the pool, so maybe falling out of a window wasn't going to hurt us.

Not like it had hurt Barclay Cargill.

It was time, I decided, to catch up with Mirela. When had she started dating an assistant district attorney, anyway? He hadn't been on her arm at the wedding; this was new. And I am always insatiably curious.

They say it killed the cat.

***

I found her in her studio.

Not right away, of course; this was, after all, August in P'town, which essentially means it will take you a minimum of three to five times longer to get anywhere than it would in, say, March. Generally by now I have a decent case of Augustitis—*please, everyone, it's been fun, now just go home*—but the week out in the solitude of the dunes had given me a different perspective. Now I could see the pleasure taken by the vacationers walking obliviously down the middle of Commercial Street; I appreciated the buskers (even the ones with limited repertoires); I smiled at visiting friends meeting up loudly and enthusiastically.

Perspective. Not a bad thing.

Mirela was working, and I don't generally interrupt her—well, to be fair, she doesn't usually let me: she'll lock the door and turn off her phone when she's concentrating. The inner door was unlocked and I knocked briefly before opening it.

Mirela was working on something propped on an easel in the middle of the room. She had covered the large sloping skylights—apparently there was a little too much sunshine for whatever she was creating—and she was wearing as much paint as she was putting on the canvas. There was a streak of magenta across her left cheek and something green in her blonde hair, providing a nice contrast. The old t-shirt—complete with holes and rips—was of some indeterminate color and design, and looked like she had done a rather inexpert tie-dye operation on it.

Mirela is Bulgarian—or was; she'd become an American citizen, possibly to offer that option to her adopted daughter Lily, now incredibly in kindergarten, the biological child of Mirela's somewhat irresponsible sister—and Mirela is still, after all the years I've known her, the most beautiful woman I've ever seen, something she carries offhandedly but is undoubtedly a help in her romantic pursuits.

She'd come to Provincetown one summer as part of a wave of Bulgarian students who arrive every year to work two or three or four jobs (you have to beware of them cycling madly from one end of Commercial Street to the other between employment venues) and party just as hard as they work. Well, they're young.

She was already an artist and spent her first couple of years doing harbor landscapes until she found her real calling, intensely emotional abstract work. I don't pretend to understand it, but it does rather grab your heart and doesn't let go: anger and love and joy and lethargy coursing through the paint and the canvas, depending on what she was feeling when she started creating. She sells insanely well, and Lily's future college and graduate-school education are already in the bank.

She didn't even glance up at me. "So the coyotes out in those dunes did not eat you," she said.

"And I didn't eat them," I said.

A quicksilver smile, come and gone in a heartbeat. "You are amusing, sunshine," she said. Mirela thinks "sunshine" is an endearment; irony and sarcasm are lost on her. Sometimes I wonder how it is we're such close friends.

I looked around and finally found a stool with only two jars of brushes on it; I moved the jars and perched. "I hear you've been busy," I said.

"I sold two paintings," she acknowledged.

"I meant your love life," I said. "Who is he?"

"And why do you think it is a man?" she countered, still with her eyes on the canvas.

It was a reasonable question; Mirela ignores labels and identities alike. The love-of-her-life-so-far was the twice-missing Guy Husband (yes, that really is his name), though she hadn't indicated a preference for his gender. "All right," I said. "Who is she?"

"It is a man," she said, her mouth twitching again in amusement. "He is a lawyer."

"I'd gathered that," I said. "Mike told me. An assistant district attorney. One I'd never heard of."

"His name is David Garratt," said Mirela. "Now you have heard of him."

I sighed. "You're in one of your moods, aren't you?"

"If you go away," she said, "you will miss the next installment of my life. There." She stood back from the canvas and looked at it critically. "I am finished for today," she announced.

"So tell me about David Garratt. And tell me what he told you about Barclay Cargill." The unfamiliar names were starting to accumulate.

She started cleaning her brushes. "He is very handsome," she said. I assumed she was talking about the live lawyer and not the dead one, though you never knew. "He thinks I am shocked by death," she went on. "I am not shocked by death. Why would I be shocked by death? But I find it is convenient for him to think so."

"Why on earth?"

"Because I can ask him many questions." She slanted me a look. "This is what you want, is it not?"

"Of course it's what I want." It's just that she wasn't usually this cooperative. "So what did he tell you? And how did you meet this guy, anyway?"

"He was with the state police when they arrived. After you and Ali left. He was interested in the scene of the crime."

Only Mirela—I swear, *only* Mirela—could get asked out on a date at a murder scene. And agree to it. You had to give her massive credit for that. "Apparently it wasn't just the scene of the crime he found interesting," I said.

She didn't pretend to misunderstand me. "I am an interesting person," she acknowledged. She still had that slight smile and I wondered, not for the first time, if I might be wrong about her sense of humor.

"And what did he tell you?" I asked again.

She'd finished with the brushes and was washing her hands, scrubbing them hard enough to take off the top layer of skin altogether. Mirela doesn't do anything by halves. "Mr. Cargill was to meet with an attorney," she said. I was starting to think there were a lot of lawyers in this story. "This is an attorney who often works with the government."

"The government? What government?"

She looked at me pityingly. "Our government, sunshine. The National Park Service."

I felt myself go cold. "The Seashore," I said.

She nodded. "He connects with Planning Design and Compliance."

"Damn." I thought about it for a moment. "Barclay Cargill wanted to develop the Seashore," I said slowly. "He was looking for a loophole so he could get development permits."

"Perhaps. His mobile was no longer with him. It is perhaps too early to imply that—"

"Infer," I said automatically. I read somewhere that hearing people use bad grammar isn't good for your heart. Maybe it was on a bumper sticker. I was ready to believe it. "But it makes sense. People could kill for that."

She wasn't fazed by my correcting her. "But will they kill to keep it from happening?" she countered. "People who do not wish for buildings to be built on the beach are not bloodthirsty people. They are peaceful. Is that not the role of the other side? The capitalists?"

I wasn't aware that anyone had been killed over land use in the Seashore. Well, at least not since Europeans had come and wiped out more than half the Wampanoag population. Still, the man *was* murdered. "What does your friend say?"

"He is not sharing that information with me," she said. She crossed the room to the freestanding wardrobe and rummaged in it, emerging with a bottle and two chipped cups. "We must celebrate your wedding," she said. "Did you drink champagne?"

"Not much." I accepted a cup and held it up while she poured. "It didn't go quite the way I'd planned," I said. "But I probably shouldn't complain. I suppose Barclay Cargill meant to spend his day differently, too."

"Cheers." She tapped her cup against mine and we drank, and I could feel the immediate rush—*rakia* is somewhere around forty percent alcohol.

Mirela refilled the cups, found a chair that wasn't too overloaded with painting paraphernalia, and sat down. "Mrs. Cargill is staying at your inn," she said. "Is there a reason you cannot talk to her? Offer her some sympathy?"

I stared at her. "Mike didn't mention she's interested in talking."

"Mike wanted you to speak to me first," she said and tossed off the last of her drink, refilled her cup, and raised the bottle in my direction. I shook my head; I didn't want to pass out on her studio floor. "It is because she does not trust the police to find her husband's killer."

"Why on earth not?"

She smiled. "She is Russian," she said. "She does not have the habit of trusting the police. This is something I understand, me. It is in the blood."

"Not trusting the police is in the blood? Whose blood?"

"We are not that different," said Mirela. "Russians and Bulgarians. We assume there is corruption in the police. It is normal. So she does not trust them. But I have a chance to speak to her, and me, she listened to."

"Because you're Bulgarian."

"Because I am Bulgarian."

I supposed it made some kind of sense. "And you told her…?"

"I told her that when you returned from your honeymoon you would help her."

"Seriously?" Usually when something like this—a corpse turning up in Provincetown— happened, no one wanted me interfering. I always did, of course, but having someone specifically ask for my help was refreshing. And slightly unbelievable.

"If you have something better to do, sunshine, I will tell her to rely on the police."

A thought occurred to me. "But isn't your—um—boyfriend the one investigating?"

"The state police are investigating," she corrected me. "David will decide to charge once there is a suspect. And you, sunshine, know this as well as I do."

"I do," I conceded. I was still getting used to the idea that someone actually wanted me to investigate something. "What's her name?"

"Galina," said Mirela. "She is in room eighteen. At your inn, sunshine."

I hopped off the stool and rinsed my cup in the slop sink. "Then what are we waiting for?"

6

Wendy Corcoran was waiting for me back at the inn.

We'd hired her as general manager after Glenn retired, giving me and Mike the ownership of the inn before moving to Amsterdam. Mike had been manager up until then, but as we each stepped into our new roles, we obviously had to replace our former selves.

Wendy was an obvious choice. She knew the business and the community: she and her ex-wife had owned a small Provincetown guesthouse for nearly ten years. When they divorced, they'd sold the guesthouse; Amelia had moved back to the West Coast, but Wendy had wanted to stay in town. Mike heard about her situation from a mutual friend at the gym and wasted no time in getting her on board.

She was loud and had more piercings than I'd ever seen on a woman—I was reminded of a line out of a Harlan Coben novel in which he describes someone as looking as if they'd fallen down a flight of stairs whilst carrying a box of fishing lures—along with about a million tattoos; but Wendy was competent, calm, and managed to stay on top of everything, no small feat with an inn the size of the Race Point in the craziness of a Provincetown summer season.

And she had a bone to pick with me. "You're not answering your phone," she said.

I hadn't checked it since we'd gotten back. "Sorry. I'm kind of out of the habit," I said.

"Mike had to leave," Wendy said. "You might want to call him. And Adrienne wants to know if you want dinner sent up to you tonight. Special treat. She'd have called if she wasn't yelling at someone at the time."

Beside me, Mirela breathed, "Who would not want it?" She was right: Adrienne the diva chef was the reason the Race Point Inn had earned and kept its Michelin rating. No one turns down an offer of a meal from her.

But there was something else going on. "What's wrong with Mike?"

"It's not him," she said. Her eyes weren't just on me; we were standing in the lobby, and she was clearly on top of the comings and goings swirling around us. "You know that girl, used to rent from him? Myra or Myrra or something like that?"

"Vaguely." Mike had washed ashore in town back when you could actually afford a mortgage, and for a long time he'd lived over across Route Six in one of the Cape Cod-esque condo communities, a two-bedroom place he could just barely afford. He'd rented the spare room over the years to a succession of people. Since then, of course, he and his partner, a veterinarian, had bought a bigger and better condo of their own. But I did remember the other place.

"Had to go to Sandwich to ID her at the morgue," said Wendy.

"What?" That wasn't what I was expecting. "What happened?"

She shrugged. "She was living somewhere in Hyannis," she said, waving her hand as though to dismiss the town altogether. "Some single-room-occupancy place. Overdose."

"And there wasn't anybody but Mike who could ID her?"

"Nobody they could find. I guess she didn't live that kind of life."

The words echoed in my head. *That kind of life.* The kind of life where people notice you, see whether you're okay, spend time with you, know your name. The kind of life, I knew, that drugs take away. "I'm sorry," I said awkwardly, though it was clear Wendy wasn't affected.

"People shouldn't use drugs," she said.

Maybe not, but major pharmaceutical companies shouldn't be pushers, either.

"Anyway," said Wendy, "the point is, he's not here, and I need a couple of signatures." *I needed them yesterday,* her tone implied. "Can you take care of it?"

"Of course." I grabbed the folder she'd had under her arm and took it over to the reception desk to sign. Grant was still there. I did a little silent self-back-pat for remembering his name. "Here you go."

"Thanks."

I was eager to be away and talking to Galina Cargill, but I strolled as nonchalantly as possible into my office. No need to advertise anything. Mirela had already wandered off, bored with the conversation with Wendy. I called room eighteen.

"Yes," Galina said, almost as soon as I'd gotten my greeting out. "Please come up."

I texted Mirela and headed for the stairs.

***

Her story, it turned out, was simple. "I told him this is foolish," said Galina, her Russian accent pronounced. "But did he listen? No. He did not. And now he is dead."

"What was foolish?" We were perched on chairs in her sitting area. Mirela had joined us, and following behind her was one of the room-service Kevins—no, wait, *John*—bringing coffee. Galina watched him pour with a practiced eye that told me that she'd once been in the hospitality industry herself.

She was in her forties, I'd guess, with bottle-blonde hair showing the roots, and more makeup than anyone short of a drag queen should be wearing. But there was pain, too, in her eyes, and even if this had been a marriage of convenience (and that was, *mea culpa*, my assumption), she had genuinely cared about her Barclay.

Mirela said, "Galina does not like Cape Cod."

"What is there to like?" Galina demanded. "There is too much sun and sand."

While I sometimes found myself in agreement with that sentiment—I tend to not be an avid beach-goer—it seemed like a diversion here. "But your husband wanted to come here anyway?" I suggested.

She took a fast sip of coffee and looked longingly at a forbidden packet of cigarettes on the coffee table. "He said it would be a vacation," she said, accusation in her voice.

"Tell Sydney what happened," Mirela encouraged her.

She set the cup down with a resounding thwack. "Instead," she said, "we come here, and it is business, business, business! Nothing but business! He has to meet with this one, he has to meet with that one. Go shopping, he tells me. Go have a manicure. We will have a nice dinner later." She stopped and glared at me. "We did not have the nice dinner, and I have not seen anything I wish to buy."

"We'll arrange for you to eat at the restaurant here tonight," I said, crossing my fingers that Martin the maître d' wasn't going to hate me forever for giving away a table. In August. We always keep one or two just in case, but they're usually for VIPs, not angry widows.

He'd have to live with it. After all, living with it was more than Barclay Cargill could do at the moment.

Mirela said, "Tell Sydney about these meetings."

Galina stood, stretched, walked to the window. She had a sort of feline grace a lot of men find attractive. Barclay had been lucky. Looking out, her back to us, she said, "Two people in uniforms," she said. "And a man in a suit. The man in the suit had a dog with him. A small, white dog." Unclear whether it was an important detail, but certainly it was a memorable one. "They met here. Not in this room, of course, in our first room, upstairs." A ripple of a shudder passed through her. "When they came, Barclay told me to go watch TV in the bedroom, or to go downstairs for a drink. But I do not enjoy drinking alone. So I go into the bedroom."

I exchanged glances with Mirela. "Can you describe the uniforms?" I asked.

Galina sighed. "They all look the same," she complained.

Mirela said, "If you wish to have Sydney to help, you must answer her questions."

Another sigh. "Dark green trousers, then," she said. "A gray shirt. Funny hats—like, what is it called, the cartoon bear?"

"Yogi?" I suggested. I was trying to keep up with my own thoughts.

"The one who extinguishes forest fires," said Galina.

There was a long pause. The ranger uniform. And the other fellow, the one with the dog, had to be the other attorney, the one who did business with the park service.

This isn't happening, I thought. So many people thought the Seashore had already betrayed the community by pulling the leases on the dune shacks, ignoring their historical significance, and trying instead to make a quick buck off them. Or as much money as possible. And yet with all the chaos and recriminations that had swirled around that situation, there was still a sense that the Seashore wanted to protect nature. Not history, perhaps; but nature.

Development on these (or any, for that matter) federal lands would change that equation—radically and permanently. There was a growing feeling of dread in my stomach. "What else can you tell me?" I asked. "Were they the only people here? Did you see anything else, their faces, maybe? Hear anything they were saying?"

She came back, sat down, and touched the packet of cigarettes. Like a talisman. "Of course I hear what they're saying," she said irritably. "You do not allow me to smoke."

"No," I agreed. "It's illegal in a building open to the public."

She shrugged, took her hand away from the packet, tossed some of the blonde hair over her shoulder. "So I must go outside." She sounded accusing.

I was startled. "Right now?"

"No," said Mirela to me. "She is telling you something."

Breathe, Riley. Just breathe. "Okay. Sorry. Go ahead, Mrs. Cargill."

Galina said, "So I must walk through the room where they are meeting," she said. "So I hear what they are talking about." She paused. "I never see the people in uniform, they are facing the other way, looking at Barclay. I have seen the man with the dog before. We had cocktails with him once. He was very—I do not know the right word—very much in a hurry. He moved fast. He talked fast."

"He was an attorney," Mirela told me. "I spoke to you of him. Barclay came to Provincetown to meet with him."

"Name?"

Both women shrugged simultaneously. "We do not know," said Mirela.

"It does not matter," said Galina.

Actually, it mattered rather a lot, but we'd get there eventually. "This is the guy who's into land planning," I said. "Who consults for the Seashore."

Mirela nodded. "Tell her what you heard," she said to Galina.

Galina said, "This man, the one not in the uniform, he kept saying, *There are ways around that. There are ways around that.* And I am thinking they are talking about real estate, and I am not interested in real estate, so I do not listen, but then Barclay says what is most important is that no one should get hurt. And now I listen, because this sounds more interesting."

She shrugged, lightly. "I do not mean to get into his business," she said. "But I am bored when he leaves me alone." She looked away for a moment, grasping her hands together; I could see they were shaking. "When he *left* me alone." I could see it hit her again, afresh, the realization that her husband was gone. Definitely, inarguably, truly gone. And not just gone, but murdered. A life stolen. No matter who he was, no matter what he'd done, he didn't deserve to be hurled through a window. And at least one person in the world had loved him deeply.

I wasn't under any illusions about the marriage. Galina's syntax was excellent, but her accent was thick. She had probably been a girl here on a tourist visa in search of a green card, and found herself a lawyer willing to marry her and expedite the process. But somewhere, somehow, they'd loved each other.

Or, at the very least, she had loved him.

I wondered how long it would be before she could sleep through the night again, before she stopped catching glimpses of him out of the corner of her eye, before she could say his name without that rush of grief and despair. How long before she started imagining a life lived without him. I wondered how she would be able to return to their home, opening the door for the first time on emptiness, feeling the rush of stale air and the echoes of his absence.

I wondered how I'd feel if it had been Ali.

There was an awkward silence, then I broke it. "I'm sorry to make you relive this."

She took a deep breath. "I want to go home," she said. "But I want to know why Barclay is dead. I want to know why someone took him away from me." Her eyes glittered. "I want to know who did it," she said. "I have to know."

I exchanged glances with Mirela; the possibility was crossing my mind that Galina had some personal, private—and undoubtedly violent—justice in mind. The possible presence of the Russian Mafia, hovering just over her shoulder, was stereotypical and xenophobic—but I wondered, all the same. Useless to speculate—we'd deal with that down the road a bit. If and when we had to.

Revenge is a common and completely understandable response to sudden loss, to grief. *You hurt me, I'm going to hurt you back. You took what I love, I'll take something you love.* I was all for justice, but I wasn't going to enable revenge. As a civilization, we've gotten past "an eye for an eye, a tooth for a tooth," or so I hoped.

The world consistently proved me wrong, of course.

I cleared my throat. "The police are investigating," I said.

"I do not trust the police." Galina's voice was impatient. "Mirela tells me I can trust you."

And why do you trust Mirela? I wondered. They'd identified a cultural connection, but how was that enough? And on the other hand… what did she have to lose? At worst, I'd fail, and the state police and the district attorney would manage on their own. "I'll do what I can," I said cautiously.

"What else do you remember?" asked Mirela, getting us back on track. "You took an interest in what your husband was saying. There was more."

Galina nodded. "The man in the suit was talking very fast. He said that it will be impossible that anyone will get hurt if Barclay follows the plan. And I am thinking, what plan? I do not know about a plan. But then Barclay says, and I think this is very odd, but he says, *And then it is over? Then I do not have to see you again?*" A pause. "And then one of the people in uniform laughed. And I must tell you, this was not a good laugh. I only heard this kind of laugh once before." She caught Mirela's eye and shook her head. "We will not talk about that other time," she said.

"It sounds like someone was threatening your husband," I said, "at the very least." *Right, Riley, let's state the obvious.* But I was still trying to work out why. Even if some sort of questionable land conveyance was the issue, even if someone had worked out how to develop multi-million-dollar homes on Seashore land, it was a matter for attorneys, not strong-arm tactics.

And yet Barclay Cargill was unquestionably dead. Maybe real estate was more cutthroat than I'd thought. It actually made more sense the more I thought about it. There are condos in town—and not very large ones at that—selling for one and two million dollars. A sale of a plot of pristine Seashore land—with an ocean view, no doubt—would be well into the tens of millions of dollars, if not more.

And people have been killed for a whole lot less than that.

The first thing, I thought, was to identify these people. And find out where they were when Barclay came sailing out of the window and into my wedding. Which reminded me... "Where were you when your husband died?" I asked Galina.

She looked for a moment as though she were about to cry, and then she pulled herself together. "I was bored," she said. "He wanted to do paperwork. Always with the paperwork. But he promised to take me to dinner in the restaurant here, and so I decided after all to go and have a drink while I waited. Perhaps also swim in the pool first. But there was a wedding, with many people outside on the patio, and even the pool had many people there, was too crowded. So I took a walk instead." She sniffed, swallowed hard. "When my husband died," she said, "I was at a bar across from the town hall, a place called Tin Pan Alley." It looked to be a toss-up whether or not she could continue. "When my husband died," she said, "I was on my second drink and flirting with the bartender."

And then she lost it altogether.

7

Mike was back at the inn by the time we'd finished comforting Galina and gleaning any more information we could from her. I caught sight of him standing at Reception, in conversation with Martin the maître d', and headed over. Mirela, her job as she saw it done, was going home to relieve her nanny.

The contrast between the two men at Reception could not have been more vivid. Martin always looks like he's headed to the opera. Mike always looks like he's planning to scale Mount Washington.

Martin excused himself and made his way back to the restaurant, and I touched Mike's arm. "Wendy told me you had to go… ID someone. What happened?

He shook his head, his dark eyes alight with fury. "Silly girl," he said. "She'd been in rehab. We thought… I wish I could've done something."

He sounded stricken, and I shook my head, wanting to immediately make things okay for him. "No. Mike, she was someone from your past, someone with a big problem, with a sickness. You couldn't fix her."

He picked some papers aimlessly off the reception desk, then put them down again. "I could use a drink."

Mike never, ever says he needs a drink. "Come upstairs," I urged him. "Great views, good company, guaranteed privacy." The latter of which would never happen in either of our offices.

I thought he'd demur; when he's at the inn, Mike's something of a workaholic—not a bad thing from the business point of view, but it takes its toll. To my surprise, after an instant of hesitation, he gave in. "Just one drink."

In the elevator he passed a hand tiredly over his face. "Do you know that Bruce's office has had three break-ins and thefts of ketamine since January?" he asked, his voice tired, resigned. He looked exhausted, sagging slightly against the back of the elevator.

This wasn't Mike. Mike had been the best manager the inn had ever had, efficient, cordial… strong. I knew better than anybody else how strong he was: one cold October, back when TransWeek was still known as Fantasia Fair, I'd been unlucky enough to run afoul of a truly murderous person who'd set their murderous sights on me. I'd ended up in the harbor with hypothermia moments away when Mike had saved me. You don't forget that kind of thing.

The elevator doors opened and I ushered him into the penthouse. Somewhere from another room I could hear classical music, Satie maybe. Definitely set the tone. "Come on," I said to Mike, pulling him along with me by the elbow. "Sit down. Breathe." My own favorite coping mechanism: *Breathe, Riley.*

It was a fairly formal living room, as set up by Barry and Glenn when they were together, before Barry's death. Glenn hadn't added too many idiosyncratic touches, and as I mentioned, Ali and I hadn't done much to change it since. But Mike seemed quite at home on the stiff satin of the Regency couch, so I relaxed. Someday Ali and I would make the place more welcoming, more "us."

I think we were still determining just what "us" really was.

I rooted around in the liquor cabinet—amazingly well-stocked considering that one of us was Muslim and didn't drink—and pulled out a bottle of one of Glenn's favorites, Lagavulin. I could smell the peaty smokiness as soon as I unscrewed the top. I poured Mike a large serving and myself a modest one, put the bottle on the coffee table—I had a feeling we'd be needing more—and sat down in what I consider the most comfortable chair in the room. Also satin-covered, of course.

Ah, Glenn.

Mike was staring into his glass, rolling it round and round on his knee. "I shouldn't feel like this, I shouldn't be taking it this hard," he said. "The truth is, I hardly knew her. Maybe that's what makes it so—so bad. I hardly knew her, but it seems I was closer to her than anyone else. She had nobody."

"What happened?"

"Fentanyl happened." He took a quick gulp of Scotch. "You know what that is? It's this synthetic opioid that's more potent than heroin, and it gets added to other drugs— heroin, meth, all that. But no one knows what constitutes a safe dose."

"So people are dying," I said.

He nodded. "So people are dying." There was a moment of silence. I couldn't think of what to say. "You should have seen her, Sydney," said Mike. "She was this little slip of a girl. Had to weigh about a hundred pounds.

You remember those pictures they used to paint for the tourists in places like Paris, those little kids with these huge eyes? That was her." He finished the drink and held out his glass; I poured some more. "And I used to give her such hell, because she could never get the rent in on time. And sometimes that was okay, but sometimes I got really irritated with her, I'd threaten to evict her out, and that's what I'm remembering."

"It's a hard population to deal with," I murmured. I actually didn't know all that much about addiction, though I certainly knew more than I wished I did. More than I wished anybody did. But my friend Garr owns an apartment in Dennis somewhere, and his tenants are always in and out of rehab, always on the edge of eviction. Even with housing assistance, it's hard to prioritize bills when your disease is claiming every dollar you have, every thought you have, every moment you have.

Every life you have.

I was aware of drug use, of course; everybody on the Cape is. I also knew that fentanyl is present in almost all "heroin" on the Cape—heroin in quotes, because so much has changed dramatically over the past five years, with fentanyl stealing the headlines in all the local papers. Every year, fentanyl's become more and more prevalent, so any "heroin" purchased has more and more fentanyl cut with it . These days, you'd be hard-pressed to find heroin on the Cape, because everyone wants—everyone *needs*—fentanyl.

In Provincetown, the drug supply leans more heavily toward stimulants, like cocaine, meth, and non-pharmacy-purchased medications like the street version of Adderall. And so everyone's at risk for fentanyl overdoses now: Up Cape with heroin, and Outer Cape with stimulants.

The Sacklers' empire of pain had stretched out to Land's End, with addictions to oxycodone multiplying, and while a core group of primarily gay men remained faithful to "Tina," their name for crystal meth—a party drug and a sexual aid, at least at the beginning—the fentanyl was starting to be their problem now too.

I could feel a headache building. Not that we hadn't already known about the drug use before, of course. Like Gloucester and Fall River—other old Massachusetts fishing towns—Provincetown had long counted on the rich fishing off the New England coast to sustain it. And it was all lovely in the garden until those banks were overfished and the federal government stepped in to make sure the fish could survive and regenerate. But their survival didn't exactly mean everyone could… and closing the fishing grounds meant ruin for many fishing families.

If the world has all gone wrong, if the lucrative jobs in the commercial fleet, once as plentiful as the fish they sought, were gone, then what did you do? If you had never been "across the bridge" off-Cape (as fully half the old-timers had never seen the need to do), then you hung out at the Old Colony Tap or the Governor Bradford, and you drank. And when the heroin coming in off the old swordfish and flounder and bluefin boats was cheaper than a decent single malt, then you tried that, too. Until you became part of the scenery, one of the walking wounded around town, hanging out in the alleyways beyond the gaze of tourists, drinking from nips bottles or smoking or shooting up, one of the ones with the vacant stares, waiting in the sun for the next shipment to come in… waiting for the ship that would never come, not anymore, not ever again.

The hard lives, the cold and the loneliness and the backbreaking, never-ending work, twenty hours without sleep, hauling in the lines, the decks awash with blood, your hands frozen from thrusting the catch into the chipped ice in the hold, the boredom, the arguments, the fights… All of that had been a way of life, accepted, grown into, loved, even… But not anymore. It was too hard now, too demanding, too much risk for too little gain.

The remnants of the Provincetown fishing fleet are all pretty much scallopers now, going out for daytrips, coming in at night. It's still hard, and there are fewer and fewer of them, with the big scallopers from Fall River and New Bedford poaching in our waters, and housing becoming more and more unaffordable.

And in the meantime, a lot of people were left behind. And the heroin flowed in. And then, after that, the oxy and then the fentanyl. Even ketamine, though that was still considered more a party drug and so claimed a lot fewer lives.

Mike's little friend hadn't been a party girl; no Special K for her. She was hardcore. And in that context, her death wasn't a total surprise.

I reached over and took one of Mike's hands away from the glass, holding it loosely in my own. "I'm so sorry," I said, inadequately, hopelessly. There would be more overdoses.

As long as the drugs kept coming over the bridge, kept coming in from offshore, there would be more overdoses.

He looked up, gave me a tired smile. "Don't know why it's hitting me so hard," he said.

"Because you're a good person."

He shrugged. "Never really knew her."

I tried for a platitude. "No man is an island."

"You haven't had enough to drink to start quoting Donne," he said, and this time the smile was a little better. I squeezed his hand and let it go. "Will there be a funeral?"

He shook his head. "No family," he said. "At least none so far. But she can't be cremated—that's Massachusetts law, apparently. In case a relative comes around later. Has to be buried." He took a breath. "I'll pay for the funeral people to transport her—it's the only thing I can do. They say she'll probably go to somewhere in Boston." He shrugged. "I'll light a candle for her at Saint Peter's," he said. "Pay for the burial or something. I don't know."

He was repeating himself, which wasn't at all like him. I wanted to tell him it wasn't his problem, but there was that whole "no man is an island" thing, and Mike's a good person. "I'm sorry," I said again.

He finished off his whisky and stood up, handing me the glass. "Thanks," he said. "At least it wasn't murder. Do you know any more about our guest?"

"I've been away," I pointed out.

"And you and Mirela have been conspiring," he said with the beginnings of a smile.

"Don't complain. You sent me to her," I said.

"Gives you something to do," he pointed out. "Wendy runs this place with an iron fist. Not much for you to get in trouble over. And, besides—"

He was interrupted by the elevator door opening. Ali came in, carrying grocery bags, looking hot and bothered. "Here, can you help—" he started, then caught sight of Mike. "Hey, sorry."

"I was just leaving," Mike told him. "Need a hand?"

"I'll help," I said automatically, crossing over to the entryway and grabbing the handles of the closest bag. "I do love a man who goes to Stop & Shop."

"I'm going to head home and see if my man did the same," said Mike. "Hey, Ali, good to see you."

"And you," said Ali. He'd tried carrying way too many bags. We managed to clear them out of the elevator and Mike stepped in.

"Mike," I said quickly, "I really am sorry."

He nodded and the doors closed. "What happened?" asked Ali.

"A girl died," I said, hefting two of the bags and taking them into the kitchen, gleaming and clean. We'd see how clean it stayed once we'd been back in residence for a few days. "Someone Mike knew years ago."

"Murder?" asked Ali. Knowing who I was, it wasn't an unreasonable question.

"OD," I said.

"Ouch." He put the last few bags on the counter and started taking groceries out. "Adrienne's sending us dinner up tonight," I reminded him. "Just in case you forgot."

"I would never forget Adrienne," he said, opening the refrigerator and putting romaine and apples inside. "So… I got a call," he said.

His voice was a little too carefully casual. I stopped what I was doing, a box of pasta in my hand, and stared at him. "No," I said. "No."

He leaned against the counter, crossing his arms. "I'm afraid so."

"We just got married!"

"And I had a week off for the honeymoon," he reminded me.

"Damn." He was right, of course; just because I could easily integrate my work with my life in general, and my murder investigations as a bonus, didn't mean he could—or even wanted to. "Have to stay gainfully employed," I said, trying to keep the bitterness out of my voice. I had no right to be bitter, not really.

"Have to do good in the world." He knew that one would get me.

I sighed. "And the world is grateful," I said. "Okay, I get it. I'm just selfish. Wanted the fairytale to last."

He pushed himself off the counter and came to stand right up against me, putting his arms around me, drawing me even closer. "The fairytale will last forever, *cara*," he said. "It just morphs."

I closed my eyes as we kissed. He was right, of course. You can't stay on your honeymoon forever—not, of course, that I wanted a life out in the dunes… but theoretically he was still right.

I hated it when he was right.

"We'll go to Paris for our anniversary," Ali said, still holding me, his breath against my hair.

I kissed him again and then pulled away. "So what's the assignment?" I asked, my voice as casual as I could make it. *Just one thing. Please don't say undercover. Please don't say undercover.*

"Undercover," Ali said.

***

My mother was, predictably, not happy. "I thought you were going to call me as soon as you got back," she said when I finally answered my phone. I have to be in the right mood to deal with my mother, but three voicemails weren't going to cut it—she'd keep trying until she reached me.

"We got back *today*, Ma," I said.

"So you should be rested," she said. "With nothing to do but get settled back in."

"Ma," I said cautiously, "you *do* remember the wedding, don't you?"

"Of course I remember the wedding!" I had to pull the phone away from my ear. Good thing I didn't have her on speaker, the whole town would have heard that. "Only the moment I've been waiting for all your life!"

"You said that the first time I got married."

"Well, this one had better last," she said darkly, blithely ignoring the fact that it was my first husband, a surgeon who'd decided he preferred an OR nurse's company to mine, who had ended the marriage. Somehow that was still my fault.

And right now, I wasn't in the mood. "I'll do my best."

"Don't you take a tone with me, Sydney Riley," she said, immediately and predictably.

"I'm not taking a tone, Ma." Of course I was taking a tone.

"Of course you're taking a tone," she said. "And what I want to know is—"

"Listen," I interrupted. "There's a lot going on here. In case you weren't paying attention, a man got killed at the inn. Which I co-own. At my wedding, which was one guest too many. And yes, before you ask, he was definitely murdered, and yes, before you ask, I am going to try and figure out who did it."

"Maybe your little hobby can wait," said my mother. "After all, you have a husband now."

Wait—what? Did she really think I was going to stop everything and devote myself to my new hubby? Was it really possible that now, as I was moving toward my fortieth year on the planet, she still had no idea who I was?

Not to mention in this case who *Ali* was.

"It's not a hobby," I said, though now that she mentioned it, it kind of was. I'd have to think some about that. Another time. "And, besides, Ali is leaving."

"What?" Yep: it didn't need to be on speakerphone, everyone within a two-mile radius had to have heard that.

"Work, Ma," I said soothingly. I managed to not point out what a foreign concept that might be to her. My mother never had much of a career of her own, and while these days she pretended to be put-upon, the truth was that she and my father—who live in an upscale Stepford Wives community in southern New Hampshire—had cleaners, a landscaping company, a handyman, and they had most of their meals delivered. What she did all day was a complete mystery to me.

Besides plan my mythical wedding, which had finally become a reality. I had no idea what she was going to do with herself now. Maybe the longing was better than the reality.

I cleared my throat. "Ali's going away for a while," I said. "And I really do have my hands full here. I have an inn to run. I want to find out why someone killed that guy."

"And interrupted your wedding," said my mother, keeping her focus on the essentials.

"And interrupted my wedding," I agreed. "So I'll probably hardly even notice he's away."

"Away? What does that mean?"

"It means he's going away for work," I said impatiently. "And, no, Ma, I don't know what he'll be doing. I don't know where he'll be doing it. I don't know for how long he'll be doing it." Based on past experience, I didn't even want to think about that. Undercover can last from one day to a couple of years. So far Ali had been away, at most, for a month and a half.

A very long month and a half.

She let that one go; for all her impatience for me to get married, my mother likes to ignore a whole lot about my new husband. She had referred to him as "that man" for at least the first year we were together; I would have loved to think it had nothing to do with xenophobia, but I wasn't going to spend too much time contemplating that. It was telling, perhaps, that my very conventional mother had not made a single remark about my not taking Ali's last name.

"Well," she said now, "we did manage to enjoy ourselves. Your father took me to dinner at the restaurant, and we had a nice long chat with your new parents-in-law."

Which was more than I'd had. Ali's parents had recently moved to Florida. I don't know that his mother was any more pleased with him marrying a Catholic than my mother was about my marrying a Muslim—though, unlike my mother, she kept most of her reactions to herself—and our ceremony had been determinedly secular.

His sister Karen, who until her retirement had been Boston's police commissioner, had been more enthusiastic. "It will be all right," she'd whispered to me before she left. "Difficult beginnings make for easy marriages." I had no idea whether or not she'd made that up, but I was grateful.

My mother, on the other hand, inspired no such sentiments. "You're not off to a good start," she said. She must have sensed me opening my mouth to say something I'd regret, for she rushed on. "And I haven't even told you! I can't believe it. Gillian's daughter Marisa is getting a divorce! And that after two children! Gillian is beside herself, of course. She never saw it coming, even though Marisa says it's the best thing for everyone involved. But Gillian said, what about the children, and that's the thing, isn't it? You can't just go running around doing whatever you want once you have a family. That's one thing to be grateful for with you, isn't it? That you didn't have children. You couldn't have gotten your divorce if you'd had children."

I closed my eyes. There were way too many things wrong with this conversation. Never mind that the divorce hadn't been my idea. Never mind that I would never in a million years have children under any circumstances. Never mind that Gillian—whoever she was, I couldn't keep up with my mother's myriad neighbors and bridge-playing cronies—clearly had no idea what was going on in her daughter's life. Never mind that it was absolutely, positively, none of my business.

"Ma," I said, "what about if I call you in a few days, when I've had a chance to settle in and Ali's gone?"

She was startled. "You don't want to talk some more about the wedding?" she asked blankly.

"No," I said. I was not now, nor at any time in the future, going to indulge in a postmortem of my wedding, no matter how much my mother was ready to go at it full tilt. She could do that with my father. Or her friend Gillian. "Ma, really, I've got to go."

"Well, Sydney—"

"And Mirela sends her love," I said quickly, desperately. For reasons I've never completely understood, and despite not understanding her art or in fact anything about her, my mother still respects Mirela. She thinks that speaking without using contractions is adorable.

Whatever works. Certainly the diversion was successful. "How nice of her!" exclaimed my mother. "And how is that lovely little girl of hers?"

That lovely little girl, my goddaughter, was one of the reasons I will never have children. Lily was more than a match for Mirela; neither of them was ever willing to back down from any confrontation.

A little like my mother, come to think of it. "I have to go," I said.

"And be sure to—"

I took a breath. "Bye, Ma."

All in all, it was one hell of a first day back from a honeymoon. And the day wasn't even over yet.

8

It was a strange feeling, coming back home, back to what passed for normalcy—the occasional murder notwithstanding, of course.

The time we'd spent in the dune shack was starting to take on an aura of unreality. It had been magical, time apart from time, the endless variations of the sand weaving their own truths that had nothing to do with streets and cars and people and issues. It was a dreamscape, even already; I couldn't imagine how I'd remember it in a year. Another place, another time, another life. The rhythms were slower, the sun more oppressive, the company more reassuring.

Real life had closed in around us with a bang.

I sat on the edge of the bed watching Ali sling clothing into a duffel bag. I was struggling to not say all the things I wanted to say, the things I'd said the first time he went on an undercover assignment, the things that made me sound clinging and insecure and frightened.

All of which I was feeling in that moment.

"I hate not knowing," I said, giving up the struggle with my worst angels. "I can't even imagine in my mind where you are."

"It's better you don't imagine where I am," said Ali.

"I know." This was all, I thought, my fault. When Ali and I met, he was working for ICE checking to see if I was enabling green-card marriages. Over time, I encouraged him to think more broadly about Homeland Security opportunities that might be more beneficial to humankind. He'd ended up transferring into the human trafficking division, which definitely counted for doing good in the world—and making me a crazy woman. Undercover in the world of human trafficking was dangerous; the stakes were incredibly high, and one misstep was enough to get you tortured. Or killed. Or both.

I had to have been insane to have encouraged him to do this. "You know that if you die, I'll kill you," I said, trying for humor, not really making it.

He paused, a pair of jeans in his hands, and smiled at me suddenly, vividly, and my heart ached with love. He was the most beautiful man I'd ever seen. And I was married to him. "I'll hold you to that," he said.

"You'd better." I cast around for something to say besides *don't go.* "Are you taking the ferry?"

"They're sending a plane."

Oh. Sometimes he took the ferry to Boston, after which he checked in with the local ICE office, got his assignment, and went on from there—wherever they wanted him to go. Sending an airplane to our relatively small airport implied a level of urgency I was sure I didn't like. "Okay," I said.

"It's going to be okay, Sydney," he said.

"I know." I didn't know.

His mobile buzzed and he checked his texts. "I have to go."

"I know." I was hating myself. I was behaving badly and I was doing it in what could conceivably be our last moments together. *Okay; let's not over-dramatize, Riley. Get a grip. He has work to do. He'll come home.*

Mirela was waiting in the lobby, a man I didn't recognize with her. He was good-looking in a kind of conventional way, and apparently suits were making a comeback in

Provincetown. "Sunshine," she said, "we are here to drive to the airport."

I shot a look at Ali, who shrugged. "Thought it might be easier if you didn't go."

"You do not want to wait for the airplane to take off," Mirela said to me. "It is better this way. We will have dinner together with you."

"I'm having it sent up." Though it was a lot less appealing now that Ali wasn't sharing it.

"Do not be silly," she said briskly. And then, as though offering sweets to a child, she added, "And we will discuss the case."

I wondered when they'd concocted this plan. But even as I thought about protesting, I realized I was suddenly, absurdly exhausted. Not at all positive I could take a protracted farewell with the TSA agent and Cape Air personnel watching curiously. "Okay," I said.

Ali raised his eyebrows. "Okay? That's all?"

"That's all." There were tears pressing against the backs of my eyes, and I was having trouble breathing. I put my arms around him and kissed him, hard and long, my eyes closed. *He's coming home*, I told myself fiercely. *He's coming home.*

He was coming home.

***

The man in the suit turned out to be David Garratt, one of Barnstable County's assistant district attorneys, and at the moment totally in thrall to Mirela. I'd seen it happen time and time again, and had gone from amazement to amusement over the effect she had on men (and women, for that matter), so this was no particular surprise.

The real amazement was reserved for dinner, of course, crafted by Adrienne the diva chef. No one but Mike (and, for reasons I'll never understand, my father) dared any extended conversations with her, but Wendy was coming along. Even now that I was part owner of the inn—including the restaurant— I tried my best to stay out of the kitchen. I limited myself to ecstatically eating her food whenever I could afford it.

I'd transferred Adrienne the diva chef's offer of room service into a dinner downstairs. Without Ali. Martin the maître d' showed us to a table and Pierre the sommelier appeared at the table to chat about pairing wines and food. He was one of Wendy's new hires and looked to be a good one.

Over the charcuterie board, David and I got to know each other. I was gentle, since Mirela is fierce enough for both of us; but by the time we'd progressed to prosciutto-wrapped figs, I was engaging less and less. Okay, so he'd gone to Yale. Okay, so he'd worked for prestigious Boston law firms before deciding that he wanted to convict criminals rather than defend them. Okay, so he had a beautiful house in Brewster and two children who stayed with him every other weekend. Enough is enough. "What do we know about the guys Barclay Cargill was meeting here at the inn?" I asked.

David looked a little surprised, but responded gamely enough. "Mirela said Galina asked you for help," he said, nodding. He'd already made his mind up about sharing with me, I thought; otherwise he wouldn't be here. More kudos to Mirela.

"Galina thinks the police will not find his killer," said Mirela. She'd lifted her wine glass to drink and now was regarding him over the rim. Almost challenging.

He was calm. "Families often feel that way," he said, taking a last bite of the figs and dabbing at his mouth with the napkin. The man had manners. "And sometimes they're right. We don't always get convictions."

"You do not always know *whom* to convict," Mirela told him. "In Bulgaria, killers are caught. And convicted."

"You're including organized crime stats there," he said. Something made me think they'd had this conversation before.

Mirela said to me, "You must know, sunshine, that very few developed countries tolerate the level of violence Americans do."

We were *not* going to get sidetracked into a discussion of gun accessibility, no matter how tempting the topic. We'd be there all night—and solve nothing. "So are you here to tell me not to help Galina?" I asked.

He shook his head. "No, actually, I was thinking that—" He broke off as our plates were removed and glasses refilled. "To be honest, I tried to convince Mirela to give me the same access to Mrs. Cargill that she's enabled for you." Odd way to phrase it, but okay. "And since she's unwilling to do that, I'd like to have your contributions to the investigation. Unofficially, of course."

"Of course," I said. The waiter (which Kevin? He fit the category, but I still didn't have much clarity around restaurant staff names) put my seared scallops with lemon caper sauce in front of me, and I almost forgot the investigation altogether.

Almost.

Mirela said, "Galina believes that there is a conspiracy."

"It's early to talk about that," said David, a little sharply. He was ignoring his duck confit, so she'd hit a nerve. No one ignores Adrienne the diva chef's duck confit.

I cleared my throat. "The question is, how did they get to be in that room together? I mean, look at who they were! There's got to be something wrong when a developer sits down with someone whose land isn't supposed to be developed." I paused. "Can they do it? I mean, really? Are there ways around the regulations?"

"There are always ways around the regulations," pronounced Mirela. "This, I can tell you for a certainty. If you can afford a bribe, there is no regulation that will stand in your way."

David was looking a little uncomfortable. "I don't think we need to make the leap to potential bribery quite yet," he said.

"Because this is not Bulgaria?"

"Because it's not the only possibility. You're right, it doesn't sound like everything he was involved with is strictly aboveboard, but I don't know the specifics. And we have investigators looking into it. Into the connections between the National Seashore and Attorney Cargill. There's never an answer until there's an answer." He caught me raising my eyebrows. "Okay, so that's trite. But it's the truth. There's always more than one way to figure things out, and if you develop a single theory of any case too soon, it leads to confirmation bias. And that's when innocent people get convicted, and guilty people go free." He shook his head. "We're trying to avoid that on our watch."

"Especially," I said drily, "as the attorney general is up for re-election."

To my surprise, he laughed. "And especially as the attorney general is up for re-election," he agreed.

"Okay. We know where we stand," I said. "But this is where I come in. Galina's willing to talk to me, and she knows a lot more than she's told me so far." A sudden idea came to me. "And I know someone who works for the Seashore. I could see if there's anything going on, rumors, that sort of thing. She might know something."

"She?"

"She's a ranger," I said. "You probably know this already, but I just spent a week out at a dune shack."

He nodded. "I heard. At Peaked Hill Bars."

"That's the one. And I met this woman— her name's Lucy O'Connell. She seems pretty plugged in to what's happening there." I was again treading carefully around a potentially explosive political issue. "And if they're going to develop, it has to be out here, doesn't it? I mean, it wouldn't make sense for them to be meeting in Provincetown if they were looking at a variance—is that the right word?—in Chatham or Nauset, right? And she's out there all the time. We saw her every day, patrolling the backshore."

Mirela frowned. "A ranger would not know," she said. "And if she is—what is the expression? What junior policemen do? Walking the pulse?"

David and I looked at each other blankly. "Oh, I get it. Walking the beat?" he suggested.

"Taking the pulse?" I said at the same time.

"The beat. Yes, that is it. A junior person."

"Maybe," I conceded. But there had been something about Lucy that had suggested she was tuned in to more than just the waves and the sand. And then there was Cyril Stephenson, who, I was willing to bet, knew a lot more about what was going on out there than he was willing to share, at least with me. To use Mirela's word, he was a guy with his finger on the pulse of National Seashore politics. And probably a lot more. "It's still worth a try," I said, and caught David's eye.

"An avenue of research among many?" I suggested, and he laughed.

"I like you, Sydney," he said. He sounded surprised.

"A few people do," I agreed, and he laughed again.

The waiter came and whisked our plates away. Mirela was looking thoughtful. "Sydney is very good at this," she said to David. "She will talk to the right people. You can be sure of that."

"The only thing I'm sure of," I said, "is that I want crème brûlée for dessert."

But of course I was sure of more than that. The question might have taken place with a defenestration in Provincetown, but the answer, I was reasonably sure, was out there in the dunes.

I was wrong, of course. But only in a way.

***

Upstairs in the penthouse, I started looking for Lucy's business card, which was like looking for a pebble. On a pebbled beach.

We'd come back from our honeymoon in the dunes dirty and sweaty and with sand in everything we owned, and Ali, the responsible one, had put all our remarkably grimy clothing in the laundry. But that had left a myriad of things to do. He'd repacked his duffel bag for his work trip and essentially dumped all his non-clothing items on one of the bedroom chairs. I hadn't even gotten that far: after piling all my belongings into my bags, I'd just dropped the bags on the floor and picked out what I needed when I needed it. Possibly not the most organized way of dealing with travel—not to mention with life—but there it was.

There was a business card here somewhere. I just knew there was.

I finally found it about a foot under the bed. I didn't have the energy to even wonder how it had gotten there, though I had my suspicions, as Ibsen was curled up beside it, looking smug. "You're not getting enough attention, are you?" I asked him. He had nothing to say in response, but managed to not claw me when I reached in for the card. "What—were you planning on making a call?"

He blinked peacefully back. If a cat could smirk, that's what he would be doing.

I sighed, got back on my feet, and grabbed my phone. Just as I was wondering what kind of disjointed message I was going to leave, she picked up. "Ranger O'Connell."

"Oh, hi, Lucy? This is Sydney Riley. We met this week—"

"I know who you are."

Okay, so much for small talk. "I hope I'm not interrupting you," I said. "I was just wondering if maybe we could have a coffee or something together, if you come into town—" Thinking of her for the first time as a real person, I realized I had no idea what she did besides patrol the backshore. Did she live in town? Did she have friends, a partner, interests outside of the National Park Service? I had a sudden vivid image of her folding herself into one of the dunes, Hobbit-style, at night.

"What's this about, Sydney? It's high season, and I'm a little busy."

Not too busy to pass the time with Cyril Stephenson, I thought, but I didn't say it. I was, after all, asking her for a favor.

And I wasn't even sure exactly what the favor was.

"Oh, sorry," I said. "Um—maybe you have five minutes now?"

"What is it, Sydney?"

I took a deep breath. "Okay. Here's the thing. I'm wondering who I should talk to about any plans the National Seashore might have for easement on building properties on federal land here. I mean, in the Province Lands." There. I'd managed to make it sound almost reasonable.

There was a moment of silence. "I don't understand what you're asking," she said. "There's no private construction permitted. Period."

"Well, that's what I thought," I said. "But I thought I'd heard of there being exceptions in the past—maybe buildings that were grandfathered in?"

She sighed. "Wait a minute, I need to sit down." There was a pause, during which I could hear her talking to someone with her hand partly over her phone. Then a clinking of glass, and another moment and she was back. "Okay," she said. "This may take a few minutes."

"I'm fine with that," I said. I was back on my knees trying to lure Ibsen out from under the bed. It was a thankless task. I gave up, silently, and got off my knees and sat on the bed instead. "Go for it."

"A little history," said Lucy, apparently deciding that the topic was worth her time. "The Seashore is unique, you probably know that. Most national parks are located in remote areas where no one had ever dreamed of building; we're the only park that was superimposed and carved into longstanding communities. And it wasn't popular, not even a little bit. We got some of the property we needed by usurping private homes using eminent domain, forcing some owners to sell and allowing some owners to stay, and don't ask me which was which because I don't know how the decisions were made, but there were a lot of bad feelings about that."

"I can't imagine," I said. I really couldn't. It didn't seem exactly fair. "What criteria were they using?"

"There were some pretty complicated one-off deals," she said. "Some long-term and even perpetual leases, grandfathered deeds. All pre-existing properties, of course. There are six hundred of them now throughout the Cape."

That seemed a lot. I didn't say anything.

"It's a unique situation," Lucy said again. "First off, there's an incredible blend of ocean, dunes, forests, ponds, and marshes, so the conditions range quite a lot among them all. But secondly, it's a unique partnership." She really liked that word. "We work with the six towns that share the Seashore as well as those private homeowners—kind of a workaround that doesn't exist anywhere else. No other property of the park service has integrated existing private residential and commercial property inside a federal wilderness. But it's also where the development issue comes in."

I was hoping it might. "In what way?" I asked.

"We'd hoped—that is, the National Park Service had hoped—that the private households inside our boundaries would live lightly on the land. They have an incredible privilege, after all." She'd managed not to say unique again. "In exchange for living inside a nationally treasured landscape, landowners were supposed to agree not to endanger Seashore resources by overdevelopment."

"And that hasn't happened?" I asked. I had a feeling I already knew the answer.

I could almost feel her shrug. "We don't have the resources," she said. "Structures don't fit into what we do, what we're best at. You've seen how we struggle with the dune shacks. We are supposed to care for nature, to care for wilderness. We couldn't give maintenance and upkeep of properties priority when you compare them to protecting nature, let alone hiring rangers and lifeguards. It comes down to money. As budgets come and go, so does what we can do." She sighed. "And already we've been overbudget for the past couple of fiscal years. We spent eight and a half million dollars in North Truro to demolish twenty-eight buildings in and around Highland Center—that's the old Air Force base and Fox

Hollow site—with another sixteen sprinkled through Eastham, Wellfleet, and Truro."

"So," I said, trying to pull her back to the question at hand, "there may be developments that slip through the cracks."

"I wouldn't agree it's safe to say that," she answered, and I could pick up on the caution in her voice, the voice that was really saying *I think it's safe to assume that.*

"It's always coming back to the money," she said. "The park service has had little and sporadic access to capital to buy new properties from willing sellers. Some towns are proposing municipal uses of park land when current owners are willing to sell, from wellfields to golf courses to wind turbines to senior centers to new beach development, and some of these facilities have been built."

"So it's possible," I said. And maybe even easier than I'd assumed. If Barclay Cargill and the so-far-nameless other attorney wanted, they could slip their proposal through the cracks. And Mirela had been right, after all; it was all about money. Have enough of it and you can do whatever you want.

And it made sense; a federal entity with a mission to protect and create access to natural habitat would by definition have a fraught relationship with human construction. That national conflict was playing out locally on the Cape, where human settlement is older than the nation itself.

But what it didn't answer was why someone would want to kill Barclay Cargill over it. A lot of people might *think*, "I'd like to kill him," but not too many people actually follow through on that thought. There was, after all, the inconvenience of prison should we follow through on our reactions to people doing bad things.

But someone had. Who? And why?

"Lucy," I said suddenly. "One last question."

"What is it?"

"How many rangers work out here? In the Province Lands, the dunes?"

"Not as many as we need," she said. "Right now? Around twenty. Out here."

I was rooting around in my memory for Galina's description of her husband's visitors the evening he died. The uniformed ones, that is. She hadn't struck me as particularly observant; but there was no reason for her to have been. She was bored and anxious for Barclay to be freed up so he could take her out. "Red hair," I said suddenly. "A guy with red hair? Kind of middle-aged?" Galina had called them old, but she was young, and anyone over forty would possibly qualify.

"Doesn't sound familiar," she said.

"But you know them all, don't you? Maybe he's just a summer hire?"

"Hardly," she said. "The summer hires are all young."

It might not, I reflected, be that difficult to obtain a ranger's uniform, or a reasonable facsimile thereof. But why would anyone want to? "The other guy was—"

"Wait," she interrupted. "What other guy?"

Might as well come clean. Maybe she could help. "You remember that man who got pushed out of a window here at the inn?" I asked. I didn't have to ask if she knew about it; everyone on Cape Cod, and probably far beyond, knew about it. "Before he, um, died, he had some visitors. Two of them sound like they were wearing rangers' uniforms."

"That's impossible," she said immediately.

"That's what I'm trying to find out. Maybe you can check the time, and see who was where? Is there some sort of centralized schedule you can look at?"

"What makes you think he had visitors?"

I didn't see any reason not to tell her. "His wife saw them," I said.

"His *wife?* Was she there when he got killed?"

"No," I said. It wasn't exactly a secret; *The Provincetown Independent* had already run two stories on the murder. "She was at the inn, but she'd gone out and saw them before she left." I felt a little breathless; I'd just had a sudden image of what might have happened, the blow that had sent Barclay Cargill tumbling down into my wedding ceremony. The uninvited guest. I'd been aware of what it had felt like to me; what I hadn't thought about was what it had felt like to be in the room.

As at least one other person obviously was.

"Well," said Lucy, oddly apparently on the same wavelength, "I hope they catch whoever did it. The poor man. But in the meantime, I'll speak to the superintendent. I don't know who those people were, but if someone's out there posing as one of us, then that's a problem. The federal government doesn't take that lightly."

The federal government. Lucy and Ali, at the end of the day, worked for the same entity. I hadn't thought of that. "I don't know if she'll want to talk to—"

"She's spoken to the police, I'm sure," said Lucy. "They might want to liaise." She gave a short laugh. "Above my pay grade, anyway. And now, Sydney, I really do have to go."

9

So by now I was pretty sure there was some significant malfeasance around Barclay Cargill's presence in Provincetown—not to mention the obvious malfeasance, probably from another direction, around his defenestration and death. And whatever was brewing, I couldn't imagine that the plan wasn't going forward even without the deceased lawyer.

Mirela was right—there had been three other people in that room, and that made it a conspiracy, *ipso facto*, didn't it? So there must be a plan in place to go ahead without him. It was still unclear to me why he'd been killed, but maybe that would sort itself out. Maybe he'd decided not to move forward with the plan. Maybe he wanted more money than he was getting. Maybe he'd decided to blackmail his partners. I was starting to feel a little like it might have been Colonel Mustard, in the library, with a candlestick.

Mike was sitting in his office doing nothing in particular when I got downstairs. "I was thinking," he said, à propos of nothing, "I might do some volunteer work."

"Oh, yes?" I sat in one of his client chairs. "Not enough going on here?" I felt there was more than enough going on here.

"Oddly enough, no," he said. "Who'd have thought?" He smiled and shook his head. "I can see now why Glenn came and went, and Barry before him, too. I never really thought about it, just kept my head down and kept going, running the place. But now, it's been a few months, and it's great, don't get me wrong, but it's definitely not the same. I mean, we get the big decisions, right? We think about five-year planning and major changes and how to stay on budget and all that." He looked a little crestfallen. "It's not like being manager," he said.

"You sound like you miss it."

"Yeah, who'd have thought?" He shook his head. "Wendy's amazing," he said. "She takes care of stuff I would have missed. She's three steps ahead of everything. Adrienne respects her." That was, I reflected, perhaps the biggest accolade; Adrienne the diva chef's respect never came easily. "I don't even check up on her anymore."

"I know," I said. He was right, of course. We had weekly meetings—Mike and me, Wendy, Martin the maître d', and (when she deigned to grace us with her presence) occasionally Adrienne the diva chef. Communication took place. Problems were solved. Our staff went its merry way and Mike and I were free to do—whatever it was two owners of a well-run inn were supposed to do.

I didn't think either of us had quite figured that one out yet.

"Well," I said at length, "we could travel."

He gave me a look. "I do have a husband," he pointed out.

"So do I," I said, a little defensively.

"Oh, right," he said, and his voice immediately became gentler. "I'm sorry, Sydney. It's rough he had to leave right after your honeymoon."

"Thanks." I sighed. "It's rough anytime he has to go undercover." I roused myself. "But that's not the point. You're bored, that's what you're saying, right?" I looked at him a little more closely, saw the line of stubble on his chin—on Ali, that sort of thing looks designer;

it just makes Mike look tired—and the redness in his eyes. "Or maybe not bored," I said, more slowly. "Mike, is this about that girl?"

He looked away from me, out the window, where sunny Commercial Street was bustling on in its own merry way. Once you stopped focusing on what was happening inside the room, you could hear voices out there, abrupt hoots of laughter, a car horn, bicycles rolling and dinging their bells incessantly, as though it were their God-given right to proceed down the street with no one in the way.

On Commercial Street in August, there's *always* someone in the way.

Mike was finding something out there quite fascinating. I waited, something I hate to do but was practicing; maybe my week out in the dunes had taught me something about patience, about slow results. Finally he drew in a very long breath, let it out, and said, "Maybe. Yeah, maybe. It's just there has to be something more than this." He his chair swiveled back to look at me. "Something bigger," he said. "We're here complaining about the heat and the tourists and people's bad manners," he said. "And we worry about the inn's margins and staffing and reputation. And meantime there's this girl who can't think beyond the next five minutes, and she's out there, just… surviving. Not wanting anything bigger for herself. Just going through the motions because it's all she has. And then she dies, and no one even notices."

"You noticed," I said softly.

"Only because they found something with my name on it in her stuff," he said sharply. "I hadn't given her a thought in years. And that's… a problem. It's bothering me. Because I'm supposed to do better than that."

"Better than what? What does that even mean?"

"*You* know," he said suddenly. "You of all people should understand. We're both Catholics. We're supposed to do good out there. No, wait—" this as I started to say something—"No matter what the so-called professional Christians are saying, you know? The politicians? The crazy people who think Jesus was pro-guns and anti-gay? We forget the reality of it because of them. We're supposed to take this stuff seriously, Sydney. Help those who need us. Welcome the stranger. Feed the hungry. Stop by the side of the road, no matter how freaking inconvenient it might be."

A couple of years ago Mike had mentioned he was going back to Sunday Mass at St. Peter's. I remembered thinking about it at the time, feeling a slight tug where he was clearly feeling a strong pull. We hadn't talked much about it since then. Maybe we should have.

Unlike Mike, I hadn't gone back, though at some level I did still consider myself Catholic. Despite the institution's obvious and glaring problems, it was still the best alternative out there, I thought: the closest to what we believed. If we believed.

I had no idea how to respond. Was he feeling guilt? Anger? It was hard to tell. "You can't change the world," I said cautiously, "You can't change people."

"No?" Okay; it was anger. "Then what's the point, Sydney? What's the point of running an inn and making sure wealthy tourists have nice vacations? What's the point of going to the gym or walking on the beach or having a drink with friends? What's the point of any of it if we can't make anything better?"

"We can't work magic." I know my voice sounded uncertain; I was feeling pretty uncertain.

"We can do better," he said. "We can do *something.*"

This girl's death had really done a number on his head. "So do something," I said. "But do it for the right reasons. Not because you feel bad about this one person. There was nothing you could have done for her. If you'd taken her in, she would have stolen from you, she would have promised you everything and done nothing. You couldn't have fixed her world. You couldn't have fixed her."

He sighed and held a hand up. "Never mind, I know what you're about to say, don't say it. It's the drugs."

I nodded. "It's the drugs," I said. "The addiction. The disease."

"So we just give up? Is that what you're saying, Sydney?"

I felt the anger building inside me, pressing on my chest. "Give up? What are you talking about? Ali is out there every day, trying to make sure people have a decent chance at a decent life instead of being used, like, like— animals." Not a good example, since Mike's husband was a veterinarian, but it was what came to mind, and I wasn't in a space to stop now. "And when I look at the results of violence here, it's not because I think I'm flipping Miss Marple, it's because I want to give them something Provincetown took away from them—their dignity. And justice."

"It's not Provincetown that took that—"

"I know, I know," I said impatiently. "But if I can find some justice, then there's some kind of meaning for them... both for them and for whoever they leave behind. And maybe make sure it doesn't happen again, no one else gets hurt by the same predator, you know? And you—you already volunteer, all *winter* you're at the soup kitchen once a week, and you did that even when you were manager here and had the weight of the world on your shoulders and everyone wanting something from you. We're all trying, Mike, whether because of our religions or because we're decent people. What were you supposed to do, adopt your tenant? Follow her around?" I was running out of steam, and his expression hadn't changed. "Okay," I said finally, letting out an exasperated flow of air. "Okay. So what's your plan?"

"What plan?"

"For volunteer work?"

"I want to learn about Narcan administration," he said, not altogether surprisingly. "I can learn it, and I can teach it. I know we had trainings here last year, but we can do more. I want every single staff member we hire to know exactly what to do when there's an overdose, and be ready to do it. I'll train people in the other inns, too. I think it's the single most immediate and important thing I can do with my time."

"It's a nice idea…" I said.

"But?" he prompted.

I shrugged uncomfortably. "As elitist as this sounds, your girl who died, she was—she was poor, Mike. She didn't have a home or a job. And that's rotten, but it's not the reality of people who stay here."

"You'd be surprised," he said. "No, no, you're right, homeless people don't stay at the Race Point. But Provincetown is a special place. And when fentanyl came in… That was a first for this part of the Cape and puts a lot of well-heeled people, both people who live here and visitors, at risk for overdose. These aren't people you'd expect to need to worry about overdoses in the first place. And that's where I fit in."

"You know where you can learn this?"

"The AIDS Support Group is more about opioids these days than AIDS," Mike said soberly. "I've been talking with Dan Gates about it. It's not a big thing, but it's what I can do."

"Then you should do it," I said. And wondered, as I did, whether anyone could make a difference. Ali clearly thought so. Mike, too.

Why was I so pessimistic about it all?

***

It occurred to me that if someone was trying to get permission, however dubious, to build trophy houses on the Seashore, then they had to have scoped out the area beforehand. More than once. Plans and maps are all well and good, and some landmarks are reasonably permanent; but the dunes are a never-ending vista of shifting sands. The "hill" you may have climbed one month ago may have changed its hollows, its circumference, its profile by the following months. Subtle changes, all of them—the real changes came in the winter, with the nor'easters and the waves pounding the shore, eroding the dune cliffs and carving out new topography—but changes nonetheless.

Someone had to have gone out there to assess the situation, perhaps even do some surveying. Figure out what could be built with reasonable safety, and where.

Lucy O'Connell had filled me in on the theory; I had a grasp of what a variance would mean for everyone who loved the bit of wild that was the Seashore. I remembered one day driving up to the Visitors' Center with a couple whose wedding I was planning, to show them around. We stood on the big deck overlooking the water, and one of the women kept going on and on (I thought) about how amazing it was to be able to see the ocean, that everywhere else—admittedly an overstatement—the land beside the beach would all be private, unattainable, the vistas reserved for the wealthy.

I didn't think much of it at the time; I'd lived out here just long enough to take it a bit for granted. But I thought about other places on the Cape, Hyannisport and Chatham and Sandwich, where you could almost believe you were on the mainland, where if you were lucky you could glimpse the sea between the estates with well-groomed emerald lawns, and I realized my bride that day was right. We need the wild.

So I had the theory. Now it was time for the practice.

And I imagined that no one knew the dunes the way Cyril Stephenson did. Not the rangers, not the nonprofits that administered some of the shacks, not anyone who wasn't out there every day, watching the shifting sands, the ocean stretching out to the horizon, the wind, and the scorching sun. Cyril, with his beloved birds, was the closest thing to someone who belonged out there, part of the landscape, staying as long as they could until migration called the swallows away and Cyril himself took up his winter stool at the Old Colony Tap.

But winter was a half a year away, and I knew he'd be out there, plugging away irascibly at his pipe, his eyes watchful, not missing anything.

Ali was away doing things I didn't want to think about. Mike was reassessing his life and priorities. Mirela was enjoying her new relationship and creating stunning emotional art. The inn itself was humming along nicely with Wendy at the helm. I put two insulated bottles filled with cold water, a hat, some sandwiches, insect repellent, and my charged smartphone into a backpack, slathered myself with sunscreen, and set off. I parked my Honda Civic—the Little Green Car, as I called it—at the Snail Road entrance to the dunes, took a deep breath and a swig of cold water, and started climbing.

Pretty much the first thing you get to when you go that route is a mountain (okay, a hill, but to someone who needs to exercise more it seems mountainous) of sand. Sand isn't easy to walk in at the best of times; add an uphill component and it can be a struggle. A triumph to make it to the top, winded and gasping, but definitely a struggle to get there.

I was feeling rather proud of myself, to be honest, as I stood there catching my breath. I could see the top third of the Pilgrim Monument if I looked back toward town; on the other side, the undulating dunes, graceful hollows, and stunted trees surrounded by odd lichens—the world of nature contrasting sharply with the efforts of people to tame it. We might end up destroying the planet, but we were never going to tame it. All anyone has to do, around here, is remember what the scenery looked like at the abandoned Air Force base out in Truro that Lucy had been talking about, the grass and trees sprouting up through the concrete. Given time, the jungle will always take over.

I made it to Cyril's shack after an hour of walking. Others would have done the distance in less time, of course, but I'd managed to get lost twice—too much of the dunes looked alike to my untrained eye—and was starting to wonder if I'd ever find the shack, much less make it back to civilization, when I stumbled upon it. Completely by accident—I'd thought I had another ridge to go before getting there.

And it was hot. My feet were sweating in my sneakers, but I'd learned during the week we'd spent out here that going barefoot in the broiling sand will burn you; I stopped once or twice to sit and empty out the encroaching sand.

Cyril was, predictably, sitting on his porch. He didn't have a pipe going, but everything else looked the same as it had the last time I'd seen him: the shack with its mismatched timbers, the scattering of birdhouses where the swallows swooped and glided, the precarious porch, and the open door into the one room beyond.

And Cyril hadn't changed, either. The weathered face with a hundred wrinkles, the faded blue eyes, the careless shorts and t-shirt: everything was the same.

Including his attitude about visitors. "You again?" he asked as I came into view, sliding slightly down the dune, trying to stay graceful and failing utterly. "Thought you'd gone back to town."

"I did," I said. "But I wanted to talk to you. Um—ask you some questions."

He regarded me, his eyes steady. "Should have your hat on," he observed at length.

I'd forgotten it. "You're right," I said, and slipped my rucksack off and fished inside. Took another swig of water while I was there, then pushed the Tilley hat onto my head.

Cyril nodded as though I'd said something profound. "What do you need?"

Not exactly a casual conversational opener, I thought. "Can I sit with you?"

"Don't know if you can."

Okay. I got it. I hopped my behind up onto the edge of the rickety porch. It had held before; hopefully it would hold again. "It's hot," I observed.

"You come out here to give me a weather report?"

O*kay*. Enough with the small talk. "No," I said. "I came out to ask you for help."

The eyebrows went up. "Help with what?"

"It's a puzzle," I said. "So here's the thing. The man who died at the Race Point Inn—he was looking to get a variance to develop Seashore land. And he was seen talking with another attorney—um, he was a lawyer himself, too—and a couple of men in uniforms that sound like park rangers' uniforms."

He regarded me calmly. "What do I have to do with that?"

"Nothing," I said. "But I thought—well, you know the dunes better than anybody, the whole Peaked Hill Bars area—and you might know where they were planning on building. I mean, it couldn't be out here, there's no infrastructure. But you get around. You see things."

"What makes you think I get around?"

"Ranger O'Connell said so. She said no one knows the area as well as you do."

He shook his head. "Don't try'n flatter me. Don't work."

"I'm not trying to flatter you," I said. "It's what she thinks, it's what she told me. And I could try and go the legal route, follow the paperwork, but that will take forever."

"And what's your interest in all this?" He wasn't looking at me anymore; his eyes were on the horizon, where sky and sea merged. A scalloper was chugging busily along the foreground, and there might have been a freighter on the horizon; it was too blurry to tell. "I don't really have one," I admitted. "Except that the inn's mine, and the man died there. I feel—I don't know, an obligation? Like I owe him something, try to find out who killed him?" I drew in a deep breath. "Listen, Mr. Stephenson, even if he was doing something—something morally wrong—even so, he shouldn't have died. Not the way he did." I paused, and Cyril didn't say anything, so I plunged on. "And it happened at my wedding," I said. "You can't forget something like that." And all the celebrating and feasting and drinking we'd missed out on, too, but it seemed churlish to add that.

He tore his gaze away from the water and looked back at me. "Seems you're something of a detective," he observed.

"Not officially," I said. "But sometimes I've been able to help." Julie Agassi wouldn't have used the word *help* to describe what I did, but Julie Agassi wasn't here.

"Hmm." He thought about it for a moment. "Lucy O'Connell send you?"

Not exactly, but I decided to go with it. "She explained about the whole legal issues around development," I said cautiously. "And of course, she's against it, but there's not much she can do in her position."

"And you think you can do more?"

I looked at him a little defiantly. At least that was the look I was aiming for. "Yes," I said.

He shrugged. "Lucy knows what she's doing," he said. "Been out here a good number of years, too, that one. Not an easy life."

"She doesn't *live* out here, though, does she?" I had a sudden image of her camping out, hanging her uniform on a makeshift clothesline. It reminded me of the assumption we all made when we were kids, that teachers slept under their desks, re-animating in time for class. The notion of object permanence wasn't a thing back at that stage of our lives.

"Lives up t'Brewster," he said. "Not an easy life. Nice Irish girl. Never really caught a break."

I'd have said Lucy was perfectly happy with her life; she clearly loved the Cape, loved the wild, loved being out in the sun and the wind. But Cyril knew her better than I did. "Why?" I asked.

"Her little boy. She didn't tell you?"

I shook my head. "I didn't know she was married," I said. She didn't wear a ring. Mine was still new enough I found myself constantly twisting it on my finger, being hyper-aware of it.

"Not married anymore," Cyril said. "Husband died, up to Dorchester, where they come from. Convenience store robbery."

I looked at him in dismay. Here on the Outer Cape, with the exception of the odd murder, most crime centered around bicycle thefts. I couldn't imagine going into a Cumberland Farms store for a gallon of milk and not coming out again. "Poor Lucy," I said.

"Happens," said Cyril, though the expression on his face belied the casualness of his voice. "Collateral damage, that's what it is. Guy didn't mean to shoot him." He paused. "Little boy was with him. Kid got shot, too, but he pulled through. Happen he has brain damage, though—never be the kid he was."

"I had no idea," I said, shaking my head. What a tragedy. A double one. "What—how is he now? The boy, I mean?"

Cyril shrugged. "They all told her to put him in a home somewhere," he said. "Not much she could do, not for something like that, that's what they all said. Before she came out here, mind you. She still lived in the city back then. Applied for the ranger program right away. She thinks the kid's better off someplace like this. State might have taken care of him, but…" He shrugged. "What kind of care would that be?"

"So where does he live?"

"With her. Lucy. She has a live-in, what do you call it, nurse's aide? Something like that. Looks after the kid when Lucy's working. Sometimes I think she's out here to escape it all. No one could blame her."

He was probably right: walking the dune cliff, looking out for the coyotes and seabirds and frogs that frequented the dunes, making sure the people who came out here respected the rules, respected nature… it all made even more sense when you thought about what it was she was escaping. Going back home would mean confronting her loss, and that of her child, all over again. "How old is he?" I asked.

"Jack? Kid's coming up on twelve. Not as you'd notice, him being feeble-minded from the brain damage an' all."

I shook my head. I was imagining all the things we take for granted. The times we meet people and make judgments about their lives without knowing what dreadful stories are in their past… and even their present. Lucy O'Connell's devotion to her job might be real, but there was an equally real financial pressure behind it, too. "You know a lot about her," I said gently.

"I think of her as a daughter," he said, unexpectedly. "She don't have nobody else, not anymore. Whatever she needs, I try and give it to her. Least of what anybody can do." He paused. "Never had a family, myself," he said. "She's closest thing I have to one. Anyway, you don't need to go tellin' her you know 'bout Jack. She keeps that part of herself to herself. Not anybody's business. But if you're goin' around poking into things, looking under the rocks as it were, you might as well know. Maybe want to mind how you go in those quarters."

I liked to think that I was always sensitive, but it was plainly not so. Not if Cyril felt he needed to warn me off, anyway. Time for a change of subject. "I won't mention it," I agreed. "But I still want to know—have you come across anything that would point to people—I don't know, *planning* something? Maybe thinking about building? Somewhere in the Province Lands?" It sounded hopelessly vague, even to my own ears. What was I really doing out here? Was I going to outsmart two experienced attorneys and two members of law enforcement who were planning—well, that was it: I didn't know what they were planning. I didn't know what conversations, arguments, misunderstandings, or changes of heart had gone on internally within their conspiracy that warranted a defenestration. I didn't know who stood to gain from Barclay Cargill's untimely death. His wife, possibly— but it was Galina who wanted his murder investigated, so there was obviously more to the story, and it had to be connected to him professionally rather than personally. Maybe. Mirela of all people was certain that there was more to it, and she had the confidence of an assistant district attorney who was working the case.

But out here in the dunes where everything is stark and bright and clear, where creatures kill in order to live, where death is a part of a cycle and motivation is survival, it all seemed to make less and less sense.

I felt more muddled than ever.

Cyril, at any rate, wasn't muddled. "You expecting a building site?" he asked skeptically. "Nothin' like that. Even if it's true, they'd want to keep it secret, like, wouldn't they? Not actually do anything until all the legal process worked its way out, crossing all the T's and dotting all the I's. Even if you're right, it could be a year or more before anything actually gets done. They're devious, them lawyers. Play it all close to the vest until the last minute."

I wondered briefly what his experience with lawyers had been; clearly not a positive encounter. For Cyril, anyway. "Okay," I said. "But you'll—you'll keep an eye out anyway, won't you?"

He leveled me a look. "This is my home," he said. "What do you think?"

I smiled. "And I'm a busybody telling you things you already know," I said. "I get it."

He looked amused. "Okay, then. We're clear," he said. He squinted up at the sky. "An' I'm late, missy, so you'd best be on your way."

"You can tell you're late by looking at the sky?"

"What am I going to do with a watch, out here by myself?" he demanded. "I know the sun. And I'm supposed to be meeting Lucy herself, up to the old Coast Guard station."

"That's a long walk."

"Why I should've set out half an hour ago," he agreed.

I slid off the porch, dusted my bottom, and hefted my rucksack. "Well… thank you for your time. And I'm sorry to have made you late," I said. "If you don't mind—I'll come out again. If I learn anything."

"Not my puzzle," he said. "Come to see the birds. We might make something of a naturalist of you after all, if you like the dunes."

I wasn't as sure of that as he sounded, but I nodded. "Thanks for everything," I said, even though I wasn't sure what I was thanking him for. Maybe for telling me about Jack. That warranted some thought.

It didn't matter; he'd disappeared into the shack before the sentence was even out of my mouth.

10

They said they could hear the explosion on Commercial Street, and even well out into North Truro as well. It broke windows at the DPW and had the TSA people at the airport on high alert.

I was just over the first dune ridge when it happened, and that probably saved my life—that, and the fact of the dunes themselves, the fact I wasn't in a confined space. As it was, the blast was like—well, I can't describe it. Maybe like being inside a tornado. Or an earthquake. I was slammed down into the sand, something screaming in my ears before the sound cut out and all I could hear was ringing.

I lay there for I had no idea how long, winded and gasping for breath, swallowing sand and coughing it back up again. In those moments I had no idea what had happened; I had no idea where I was or even, for a few terrifying moments, *who* I was. The bright hot day had gone dark, and I wondered if I'd been blinded by whatever had just happened.

I think I knew already in my heart what had just happened.

For all that the dunes had for centuries been the home of lifesaving endeavors, there was no way modern town fire equipment could make it out there. It didn't really matter; there were no other buildings nearby to become inflamed, and—I realized this once I struggled to my knees and crawled back up the slope of the dune—no way that anyone inside the shack had survived.

Cyril Stephenson, whom I'd been talking to three minutes before the blast, dead, his shack in flames.

I had tears streaming down my face and found myself screaming incoherently, with no one around to hear. The reality of who was there in that fire had hit as soon as I came to my senses and remembered what had happened. I might be playing a little Agatha Christie here and there, but I almost never knew anybody who got killed. *It must have been the propane stove*, I found myself thinking; and, *Breathe, Riley. Just breathe.*

Not the easiest thing in the world to do. My lungs felt as though they, too, were on fire.

The hikers who arrived first kept talking to me, and I could see their mouths moving, but I couldn't hear anything. Oddly enough, this didn't really bother me; I felt removed from everything around me, like some rain-streaked pane of glass had encircled me, keeping everyone and everything at a distance. I was aware of other things, too, but only gradually, as if only one sense at a time could take anything in. The heat, the enormous heat thrown off by the fire. The blinding brightness of the flames. The taste of metal in my mouth from the adrenaline surge. The hikers, anxious on their phones, motioning me to sit down. The sand under me, hot from the sun, burning.

Eventually more people came. I sat and watched the shack burn, moving back only when an EMT helped me up and made me totter away; there were still small explosions popping off inside the flames, and I thought of our week in Louis's dune shack and all the flammable things there, the propane, the wood stove, the picturesque kerosene lamps.

I'd started hearing again, but the voices were distorted, the way you hear things under water, and I stopped trying. I was shaking and cold and scared and felt that I really didn't care what anybody was saying. They got me to one of the over-sand trails and there was an ambulance waiting there, its tires partially deflated to be able to drive in the dunes, another EMT waiting, getting me into the back and laying me down, tucking one of those thin metallic blankets they use for emergencies around me.

I must have lost consciousness after that, because while I was vaguely aware of lying in the back of a vehicle, I didn't take much of it in. The adrenaline spike was gone, leaving me exhausted and numb.

I don't think I really got it until I was in the emergency room at Cape Cod Hospital in Hyannis, an hour away from Provincetown, and the EMT was talking about me, and literally over me, to someone on staff, and I was so grateful that my hearing was returning that I complained loudly—far too loudly, I had no idea how to moderate my voice at that point—about them speaking of me in the third person.

"That," said a familiar voice, "sounds more like the Sydney Riley I know."

I closed my eyes. "Not you," I said. "Not now."

"Oh, it is now," Julie Agassi said. Just what I needed. My own personal police detective.

They held her off for a bit while they attached various things to my arms and chest, taping the needle in my vein for whatever it was they put in the saline solution drip. Someone shined a bright light into my eyes and told me to look in various directions, and someone else started putting something on my skin that hurt like hell. Later, I understood they were cleaning the various cuts and contusions I'd sustained; at the time, it just felt like busy insects were swarming around me, biting and stinging.

And then they cranked up the bed so I wasn't quite lying prone, and Julie's face swam back into my field of vision. "You're still here," I said resignedly.

"Don't worry," she said. "Pretty soon there will be a lot more people asking you a lot more questions."

"Something to look forward to." I licked my lips; they felt cracked. "Can I have some water?"

She held the cup and straw for me, which was the most maternal I'd ever experienced her, and it scared me. "Am I dying?" I asked. "Is that why you're here?"

"You're not dying, Sydney. Don't be over-dramatic." But there was relief in her voice. "I need to ask you some questions."

"Of course you do. When haven't you wanted to ask me some questions?"

"Stop getting involved in mayhem, and I'll stop questioning you," she said. "It's pretty easy. What happened out there?"

I wet my lips again. "I was talking to Cyril," I said. "Cyril Stephenson. He…" He was dead. I had just been talking to him, and now he was dead. "What happened?" I asked Julie. "Did the stove do this?"

She ignored me. Julie's pretty good at ignoring me. "Why did you go see him?" she asked.

"I thought…" I couldn't remember what I'd thought, or even what we'd been talking about. Something about my hat? That couldn't be it. "I don't know," I confessed. "I can't remember. I remember walking out from Snail Road… I wanted to see him. I don't remember why."

"That's normal," she said, though she didn't look any too happy about it. "It will come back."

"It *may* come back," said someone else, and I turned my head and saw a young woman in scrubs checking my drip. "Don't try and force it," she said to me. "Some memory loss is associated with traumatic events. You might remember, you might not."

"*Thank* you," Julie said to her. "I don't think Ms. Riley needs anything else right now." Julie hates people contradicting her.

I said to the nurse, "My head's hurting."

She nodded and checked the chart clipped to the end of my bed. "I'll get you some Tylenol," she said.

"That's disappointing."

She smiled. "We don't like giving anything stronger. You should know that you have a mild concussion. It's going to hurt for a while, I'm afraid."

Julie said, "Are you finished now?"

The nurse was unimpressed, which impressed the hell out of me. Julie can be scary. "I'll be back," she said to me, and retreated somewhere into the center of the emergency room; the beds were all clustered around the cubicles in the center like satellites around a mothership. Who needed drugs when my own thinking could go off on tangents like that all by itself?

Julie sighed and pulled a chair over to sit beside me, her ubiquitous notebook at the ready. "Can you remember if anyone else was out there with you?"

I shook my head on the pillow, which was a mistake, the pain inside it seemed to sizzle.

"No. I don't think so. Just Cyril and me. I think."

"Anyone else around? Not necessarily with you at the shack, but anywhere else in the immediate environment?"

I didn't move my head this time. Contrary to popular opinion, I *can* learn from my mistakes. "Some people came," I said uncertainly. "Two people, I think? After the—after it happened, I mean." I paused. "I think they called you. Did they? Did they call you?"

"Were they present before the explosion?" She didn't have any problem saying the words. Then again, she hadn't been the last person speaking to a dead man.

"I don't think so," I said. "I think it was just us." I giggled suddenly. "And the birds," I said.

"The birds? What birds?"

"The swallows. There were birdhouses on stilts all around the dune shack. He loved the swallows." A thought pierced through. "Are they all right? The birds?"

"I don't know," she said. She clearly didn't care. "Did you see anyone else?"

"I don't think so," I said again. I wasn't sure of anything I might or might not have seen. I was still thinking about the birds. "They die of smoke inhalation, don't they?"

"Who?" She looked a little startled.

"The birds. The swallows," I said impatiently. "They were dropping out of the sky. I remember seeing that on the news. Years ago, when they were reporting on the wildfires in Australia. They said the birds were burning. Burning, and dropping out of the sky."

Julie was starting to look at me with concern, the way she might have looked at an elderly relative who was talking about spaceships landing in the backyard. "You need to rest," she said, her voice—for once—uncertain.

The privacy curtain twitched, and Mirela burst in. "You are alive!" she said to me.

"It seems so," I agreed.

Behind her was—Dave? Bill? Ben? I couldn't remember his name, one of those short nicknames men seem to like. The new boyfriend.

The assistant district attorney.

That was why Mirela was here; I couldn't imagine them letting her into the emergency room otherwise. But Julie and—what was his name?—had the right to be there, they were official. God only knows who they'd said Mirela was.

She had a hand on my forehead. "Are you in pain, sunshine?" she asked, then went on without waiting for an answer. "You are all right. This is the best news." She looked away from me as if noticing Julie for the first time. "She is all right, is she not, detective?"

Julie said, her voice dry, "It would seem so."

Mirela pulled her attention back to me. "David is here, sunshine," she said. "He wishes to ask—"

"David," I said loudly. "That's right. That's his name. David."

Mirela said, "Where is your doctor? There is something wrong in your head, sunshine." She looked around. "I do not see any doctor here." Her voice was accusing.

"You could go look for her," I suggested. Mirela's level of manic energy was a little too much for me right now.

David Garratt cleared his throat. "How do you feel?" he asked me.

"She was in an explosion," Mirela told him. "How do you think she is?"

"She wasn't in an explosion," said Julie. "She was *near* an explosion."

David ignored them both. "I'm interested in speaking with you about it." He glanced around, but Julie wasn't giving up her chair. "Do you remember seeing anyone around the dune shack prior to the explosion?"

I shook my head. "I don't remember much," I said. "But…" A thought was working its way slowly and dimly through my brain. "Why are you both here?" I asked. "What happened out there? It was the propane, wasn't it?"

There was a crossfire of startled looks. "We're not making any assumptions at this time," said David carefully. "We're not taking anything off the table."

Mirela said, "I am going to find this doctor." But she didn't leave my bedside.

"Your memory may come back in stages," David said to me. "Don't try and force it. That never helps." I could sense rather than see Julie shifting on her chair; there was definitely some history there. And not a good one. "But if you can remember anything, let me or the state police know." He produced a business card and put it on my tray table.

"She'll call me when she remembers something," said Julie.

David glanced at someone else outside the privacy curtain. "Or, he said, "you can talk to the agent from the National Park Service Investigative Services Branch." His voice was dry. "Hello, Adam. Didn't realize you were on-Cape."

Another uniform. Another face I didn't know, another name I didn't know. "This is ISB Special Agent Parker," David said to me. "He works for the national parks."

I giggled. "A park special agent called Parker," I said.

The special agent wasn't amused. Like I said, it's the first thing they teach at the Academy. Any law-enforcement Academy. "Ms. Riley. It looks like you have a full house here. I'm going to want to speak with you soon."

"What blew up?"

He frowned. He wasn't used to witnesses demanding information. "The investigation is ongoing," he said stiffly. "Here's my card. I'll be in touch with you tomorrow when you have had a chance to rest." He gave a careful glare in the direction of both Julie and David.

I wasn't interested in their territorial disputes. "You think someone did this deliberately?" I asked the cubicle at large. I didn't wait for anybody to say anything. "That's absurd. This is an old man who lives alone." With the birds, I wanted to say, but that hadn't gone over very well with Julie before. "Who would want to kill him? No one would want to kill him. He's a little opinionated, but that's all. He's—he was—

no—no danger to anybody." In my experience, being a threat to someone else—their family, their finances, their love life, their liberty—was one of the best motives for murder.

I'd never become a blackmailer. That would be just asking for someone to come along and bump you off.

"Like I said—we're not making any assumptions yet," David said.

Mirela asked impatiently of no one in particular, "There is no doctor in this hospital?" She twitched the privacy curtain but still didn't leave. I had a feeling she didn't want to miss anything.

"I can't help you," I said, aiming my remarks at the air somewhere between Julie, David, and the federal agent. "I don't remember anything." Just the searing heat, the force slamming me down into the sand like a giant throwing my body about, the fear that I wouldn't be able to hear again. Just the knowledge that Cyril had gone into that cottage and hadn't come out. Just the earth moving and still moving and not wanting to stay still.

What had we been talking about? Why had I hiked out to see him? I must have had something important to ask—Cyril wasn't the kind of person you just drop in on for a cup of tea and a long comfortable gossip. Why had I gone out to the dunes?

And did it have anything to do with the dune shack exploding?

Julie sighed and stood up, stowing her notebook in some inner pocket. "You can call me," she said to me. "See if you can remember anything." She looked at David and the guy from the ISB. "And until then, the question of jurisdiction is open," she said. "The district attorney already has one homicide in Provincetown to investigate."

"And now I have two." David caught her look, and almost smiled. "Come on, detective. You don't think for a moment that the two aren't connected."

"We're not making any assumptions yet," she said, tossing his words back at him with a smile that—amazingly enough—I could only describe as sarcastically sweet. Not Julie's usual style at all. Well, maybe the sarcastic part.

It was all very interesting, but my own questions were still banging around in my head. And the nurse still hadn't returned with my Tylenol, either. Too much law enforcement around, maybe. Not everybody is comfortable around cops.

I leaned my head back and closed my eyes. Maybe they'd take the hint. Even if they didn't, I wasn't in the mood for any more conversation. I needed some silence and solitude right now to try and work this out in my head.

Mirela finally went and found someone she dragged back to my cubicle. "I brought her clothes," she was saying. "She cannot stay like that. Her dress is ripped."

The nurse started to say something, but my money was on Mirela for an override, and I was right. "She needs you to look after her," she said. "Please do what it is your job to do."

I didn't open my eyes, but I still smiled. She said, "And do not look so smug, sunshine, or I will not offer to call your husband."

There it was, that word again. I opened my eyes. There's a magic number they give to families of undercover agents. We can't call them directly in the field, of course, but the agency gives us access to a staffed number; we're not supposed to use it for anything trivial, but we can leave messages if something important or unforeseen arises.

I was pretty sure this qualified.

"Tell him I'm fine," I said.

"You are not fine, sunshine," Mirela said, "but I will say that you are." She glared at the nurse. "You need to make sure she is fine until she can go home. When can she go home?"

The poor woman cleared her throat. "We want to keep her for a few hours," she said. "She has a concussion. They want to do a CAT scan. If everything's clear, then—"

Mirela had whipped out a card and dropped it on my tray table next to Adam's and David's. Great, now we had dueling business cards as well as law enforcement people. "Call me on that number," she said to the nurse, "as soon as you know. I will come and bring her home."

The nurse nodded meekly. Wise woman.

I asked the only question I was pretty sure they might answer. "Is anyone besides me hungry?"

***

They gave me a lot of time to think. Wheeled me down various far-too-well-lit corridors into various rooms for various tests, and finally brought me back to Emergency, where I got to stand up and realized, for the first time, how many bruises covered my body. "You were lucky," said my nurse.

"Yeah, I'm starting to think so."

She helped me into the shorts and t-shirt Mirela had brought me, assured me that someone was on the way, and watched me go with absolutely no impression that she was going to miss me. I'd disrupted the hospital routine long enough, was the message I was getting.

That was okay. I had no desire to be part of its routine, not then, not ever.

It wasn't Mirela who pulled up to the entrance, but Mike. In my Honda, known far and wide as the Little Green Car. I frowned at him. "What are you doing here?" Yeah, okay, stupid question, but I was still feeling pretty disoriented.

"Getting you back safely," he said. "Come on, get in." He came around to my side of the car and started to ease me in. "I am not an old lady," I snapped at him. "Can manage just fine on my own."

He held up his hands in mock surrender. "As you wish, princess."

"And don't go quoting movie lines at me, either." I managed to get my seatbelt fastened and leaned back, closing my eyes as he got back in behind the wheel. "Sorry, Mike. I'm feeling pretty peevish."

"Who wouldn't?" He started the engine and guided the Little Green Car out of the parking lot. "Don't scare me like that again," he said, conversationally. "You're only allowed to risk your life if I'm around to save you."

Which, to be fair, he had done on more than one occasion.

"Promise," I said.

"Hmm." He drove for a few minutes in silence. We were nearing sunset and the long summer night stretched out before us; but the solar glare at this angle was blinding. I fumbled around in my glove box for sunglasses and came up with an envelope.

Mike glanced over. "What's that?"

"Haven't a clue," I said slowly. I never look in my glove box; it could have been there for months. Years, even. My name was on the outside.

I ripped it open and gasped, automatically pushing it away from myself. "What is it?" said Mike. "Sydney? You all right?"

I took a deep breath, picked the paper back up from where it had fallen to the floor, and turned it to face him. He pulled over to the side of the road, prudently, and took it from me.

It was like one of those old-fashioned ransom demand letters, literally cut and pasted from a magazine. And we looked at each other over the words.

INVESTIGATION CAN BE MURDER.

"I guess," I said tiredly, "we'll have to call Julie, after all."

***

Mike drove my car down into the inn's underground parking, and we got out. "I'll have something sent up to the penthouse," said Mike. "You can just go straight up."

It sounded like a good plan. I was tired and hurt all over, my muscles aching the way they might when you have the flu. But I'm nothing if not a masochist, and thought I should probably at least show up in my office. I might not have really yet gotten my arms around what precisely I was supposed to be doing as a new co-owner, but I was pretty sure not showing my face wasn't one of those things. Absentee owners are more and more a thing in Provincetown, where corporations are buying up inns and restaurants, and it was important to me to show that the Race Point Inn wasn't one of them. That I wasn't one of them.

I didn't make it all the way to the office; Mirela waylaid me and dragged me into the smaller bar by the lobby, the one that had nothing to do with the restaurant, where evening service was in full swing. "Don't you ever go home?" I asked her crossly. "One would almost think you're the one who works here, not me."

"One would almost think," said Mirela, "that you are not interested in solving Galina's husband's murder. I am here to remind you."

"I never knew Galina's husband," I said. "I knew Cyril Stephenson."

She got me ensconced on one of the more comfortable barstools and gestured toward the bartender. I automatically wanted to call him one of the many Kevins, but reminded myself that he worked for me now. Jonathan… Jack. That was it: Jack. "She will have orange juice," Mirela told him. "I will have an espresso martini."

"Orange juice?" I asked her when he'd moved away.

"You have a concussion," she said. "You cannot drink alcohol with a concussion."

"Maybe not, but it would do my nerves a lot of good."

"You need to focus, sunshine," she said. "The state police are not getting far."

"Wait until they hear the latest," I said drily. Mike had taken the letter to the police station.

Jack brought us our drinks, and I thanked him by name. He gave me an amused smile as he moved away to take someone else's order, and I thought I'd probably gotten the name wrong after all. How had Glenn kept up with all these people? How did Mike, or Wendy? "Okay," I said to Mirela, but the truth was I was in fact having trouble focusing. Galina… Barclay… they seemed like names from some half-forgotten movie I'd seen in the past. Cyril and the explosion and the darkness that had wrapped around me in the middle of the day seemed so much more real.

I wasn't sure I could do anything about any of it. "Did you call Ali?" I asked. Thoughts were moving through my head at the speed of light, most of them as unconnected as I felt. Ali… it would have been really, really nice to have Ali here right now.

"I left a message on the magic number," said Mirela. "I said you are unharmed."

I sighed. No sense in trying to work out whether the message had gotten to Ali, or whether he was in a position to call me… I just wanted him to know. It felt less scary, knowing he was somewhere out there, knowing what had happened.

And, I reminded myself as I sipped the orange juice, whatever fears or ill effects I was experiencing, what had happened hadn't primarily happened to me. It had happened to Cyril. "I wonder if he had any family," I said, suddenly, to Mirela.

"Who? Ali?" Not unsurprisingly, she hadn't been inside my head for the last few moments.

"No. Cyril Stephenson. The man who—whose dune shack got blown up."

She shrugged, indifferent, and sipped her martini. "I do not want you to forget Galina," she said.

"Probably Lucy will know," I said. We were having two completely different conversations, but it didn't seem to matter. Everywhere I looked, there was someone who was relying on me to find out something, and I'd done little but run around in circles. I still didn't know why I'd been out at Cyril's shack. I still didn't remember what we had talked about—or if we'd talked at all. It was beyond frustrating.

"Listen, sunshine," said Mirela at last, "I must go home. Lily's nanny will quit one of the days like this one." She downed the rest of her drink in a single swallow, a feat I'd have admired had I not seen it dozens of times before: the girl could hold her liquor.

I was wondering if I should call Lucy, or whether that was inappropriate; my confusion was nothing next to the grief she must be feeling.

"Go," I said, and waved Mirela off. "I don't know why you were here, anyway."

She slid off her barstool and came over and gave me an awkward half-hug. "To be sure you are all right, Sydney, why else?"

"Thanks, Mirela. I'm fine," I said.

But I wondered in my heart of hearts if that were really true.

11

The next morning all the bruises were setting up a chorus of aches all over my body. Secret agents in thrillers were constantly getting blown up, or beaten up, and none of them ever moved as delicately as I was doing.

Maybe I wasn't meant to be a secret agent.

Speaking of which, a text had come through in the night from a number I didn't recognize. "*Cara*, take care, glad you're okay. See you soon." Ali had found a way to be reassuring even though he was off doing his own secret agent thing, and I was still smiling over that when I made my way to my office downstairs.

Everything at the inn was normal. Tourists coming and going; guests for the fabulous brunches the restaurant offered in season; groups of friends already out in the pool or lounging around it; an overweight middle-aged couple in Reception wanting to know what we do with the Pilgrim Monument in the winter.

In other words, normal.

I swallowed some ibuprofen and checked my inbox, dealing with the lowest-hanging fruit. The new events manager, Jamie, asking about a fall wedding. Adrienne the diva chef reminding me that she was going on vacation in September (Martin the maître d' was probably already getting a headache over that one. I'd leave him to it unless he asked for help.) A note from the veterinarian reminding me that Ibsen was due for a check-up—easily deferred, as there would be howling and blood involved and I just didn't have the energy.

And then an email from the offices of Andrew Young, Esq. I hovered the mouse over that one, not quite daring to click. We're an inn. Things happen here, no matter how hard we try for them not to. A guest slips on the stairs; a car gets dinged in the garage; that sort of thing. People look at the Race Point Inn and assume we have deep pockets out of which might just come some riches for themselves. I remembered once, many years ago, when I'd first come to work here and Barry, the inn's former owner and Glenn's partner, had been opening a letter from an attorney. "Someone's suing us," he said.

"For what?"

He frowned, smoothed the paper. "For not bringing them extra towels."

"You're kidding! They can't—no one can sue for that, can they?"

"People can sue anybody for anything at any time," Barry said cheerfully. "Keeps the lawyers gainfully employed, anyway."

Now as I clicked on the email I was vaguely expecting something similar. Someone somewhere felt we had wronged them somehow. I'd have to get Mike involved; he knew who was representing the inn. I had no idea.

And then I read the email.

***

He came over at lunchtime.

He wasn't far from middle age, wearing chinos and a polo shirt, which belied the fact that he was a lawyer; they get to violate the no-suits-allowed fashion rule on the Cape, and most of them do. He also had a dog with him, and Martin was on that right away. "Sorry, sir," he said, smoothly inserting himself between the man and the restaurant. "Board of Health rule; we cannot allow animals in the dining room."

"I'm here to meet Sydney Riley," the lawyer said. He might as well have been wasting his breath. Martin wouldn't have cared if he were there to meet the pope; his dining room was his domain, and he ruled it with an iron fist, albeit one gracefully covered in velvet, of course.

I decided to put an end to the contretemps. Besides, my head was hurting again and I was happy enough to go somewhere more quiet. I came up behind Martin. "Mr. Young?"

"That's right." He turned to me with something like relief. He was holding the dog, something small and white, and he added, "She's deaf. I can't just leave her alone…"

"Of course not." I gave him an encouraging smile. "Martin, we'll have lunch in the lounge, that should work out okay."

Martin acquiesced, handing me two menus and turning smoothly to the next guest. "Good afternoon, sir. Do you have reservations?"

I slipped past him and gestured for Andrew Young to follow me. In the small lounge I lowered myself carefully into an armchair while he and the dog took the sofa. "Her name is Patience," he said.

I wasn't sure what I was supposed to do with that information, so I nodded noncommittally and offered him a menu. We settled on lunch—gazpacho and a salad for me, our famous charcuterie platter for him—and then I eased myself farther back in the chair and the bruises sent up a muted chorus of dissent. "You wrote," I said, "that you know something about Barclay Cargill."

He nodded. "I do. We were colleagues. Well—" he stopped himself, as though mentally fitting the words together before they came out of his mouth— "not at the same firm, you understand. But we had dealings with each other over time."

"I see." I looked at him warily. I was *feeling* pretty wary; the moment I'd read that name in the email I felt I was standing at a precipice of some kind. This guy might have the answers.

He also might have thrown his colleague out a window. It cut both ways.

He put the little dog down on the carpet, and she snuggled happily by his feet. Of course he hadn't thrown anyone out a window. Dogs wouldn't trust someone that nasty.

"It's my understanding that the state police want a conversation with me," he said. "I was with Barclay the evening he was killed."

Okay, so maybe some dogs can have bad taste. Even deaf ones. The guy I'd been trying to identify had just walked into my hotel and admitted the police wanted him for questioning on top of it. That argued for a fair bit of daring.

And then it hit me. The dog. "You were in his suite," I said. "You and two other men. National Park Service rangers."

He looked slightly confused, but nodded. "I was there," he said again. "I left before—before Barclay died. I'll be telling that to the state police this afternoon. But I know you're in touch with Galina Cargill, Barclay's—er—widow, and—well, it's really important that I speak to her."

"To tell her what?" That you didn't kill her husband? Sounded a little thin.

"Barclay left me something." He wasn't maintaining very good eye contact; pop psychology would have a lot to say about that. "Not in his will, nothing like that. But something that's important to me. And I believe Galina has it."

"She probably has all his effects," I said. "But—"

There was a knock at the door and another of the Kevins—no, damn it, this one's name definitely was Anthony—came in with our lunches. He delivered the food to Andrew on the table beside the sofa, and to me on the chair to my right. I didn't chance using his name. "Anyway," I said as the door closed behind him, "she'll have someone to sort that all out, won't she? Unless you're the family attorney?"

Andrew was busy feeding a piece of cheese from his platter to Patience, who was living up admirably to her name. "I don't practice estate law," he said.

"No," I agreed. "I didn't think so." Who had told me about it? Mirela? Mike? "Property development and land use," I said, watching Andrew.

If he felt discomfited by my knowledge, he certainly wasn't showing it. "Pretty much," he agreed, adding butter to a piece of crusty French bread and chewing ruminatively. He swallowed, took a sip of mineral water, and fed Patience a bit of cured meat. "But it isn't anything to do with that," he said. "What I'm asking about. It was something personal—I know Barclay wanted me to have it."

I wasn't ready to move on. "The two of you," I said, "had some sort of plan to build on Seashore property." I was pretty sure that's what Mirela had been getting at, and Lucy had confirmed it. "That's my property, too, you understand. It's the property of everyone who pays taxes in this country. Isn't there enough development already on the Cape? Why do you need more?"

He looked at me blankly. "For money, of course," he said, clearly baffled by the question. "Why does anyone do anything?"

Silly me. "So what happens now?" I asked. "Is the project still on, even though Barclay's dead?"

"It's unclear," he admitted. "It'll probably take more time, more effort, more cash." He shrugged. "I'll work out something," he said. "But that's not what's important right now."

I'd finally had a mouthful or two of gazpacho, and I patted my lips with the napkin. Even that hurt. "Whether or not you find a way to build on protected land might not be important to you, but it's important to me," I said.

What was important to me was clearly not his concern. "All I need is for you to find Galina, and persuade her to talk to me," he said.

I stared at him. This laissez-faire attitude about destroying property, not to mention the death of a colleague, was getting to me. "And why should I do that?" I demanded. "Listen, Mr. Young, in the past few weeks I've planned and taken part in a wedding—mine, in case you're interested—which was cut short by the murder of your associate. I've made friends with someone who literally got blown up yesterday, and I nearly went with him. I've received what I consider a threatening letter. My husband is away, and my best friend is pushing me to find answers. Honestly, after all that, what you want and don't want is way far down on my list of priorities."

"I'm sure," said Andrew Young, "that we can come to some sort of arrangement."

"For *money?*" I could barely get the words out. "You think I'll help you for money?"

He was completely unruffled. "Most people do," he said.

"I won't," I said.

He didn't seem the least perturbed. "I think they call that virtue signaling, these days," he said. "What we used to call claiming the moral high ground. Either way, it's a little too much for someone in your position."

"And what position is that, exactly?"

"I'd think you'd know. Your husband is an ICE agent."

"And?" I bristled. Along with everything else there was to dislike about this guy, it was extremely creepy that he knew so much about me and Ali.

"They're famously corrupt."

I was on my feet, bruises be damned. "My husband is not corrupt," I said. "He does so much more good in one day than you've probably done in your whole life, and for you to suggest anything else isn't just ludicrous, it's slanderous." Belatedly I hoped I'd gotten the right word; I can never remember which is which, between libel and slander. Certainly not when talking to a lawyer. One who had already shown me what level of compassion I could expect from him.

Andrew wasn't even bothering to look at me. "It would be unfortunate," he said, "if your paragon of an honest ICE cop were to find himself embroiled in an ethics mess." He glanced up from petting Patience. "It might take him away from—what was it you called it? Doing so much more good in one day than I have in my lifetime?"

I had gone cold all over. "You couldn't," I said. "It's nothing to do with you."

"And it will continue to be nothing to do with me as long as you bring me to Galina Cargill," he said.

I stared at him. I honestly didn't know what to do. "You're threatening to set Ali up for some kind of—of bad behavior—unless I do what you want me to?"

He lifted his shoulders slightly. "It's such a small thing to do," he said. "Just one introduction, really, and Special Agent Hakim can go about his business. He's undercover at the moment, isn't he? It would be even more unfortunate if that assignment turned bad. Maybe even dangerous." He scooped up the dog from the floor and stood up. "A lot of mess and potential violence that could be avoided. And as you pointed out, you have a lot on your plate right now. So let's just go see Galina, and it will all be fine."

I couldn't think quickly enough to get in front of this. He was good: as soon as he saw his go-to ploy wasn't happening, he immediately found another pressure point for me. I had no idea whether or not he really had any way to compromise Ali's investigation—or even put Ali himself in some kind of danger—and I couldn't afford to assume it was bluster. He was sounding like someone out of the Mafia, not the legal profession, and I wasn't taking any chances.

I walked over to the door, opened it, and stood aside. "If you'll let me know where you're staying," I said, "I'll ask Galina if she can meet with you, and I'll let you know."

He didn't move. "That's not enough," he said.

"It's what you get," I said. "Look, you already know she isn't staying here anymore, she checked out, and I'll have to find her before I can ask her anything." Well, that was true as far as it went; I knew exactly where Galina was: staying in the guest room at Mirela's house on Franklin Street. Possibly not the cleverest of hiding places, but who knew she was going to need to hide?

And what on earth could Galina have—not information, something physical, something concrete—that Andrew Young could want?

"In that case," he said, "I think I'll just avail myself of the Race Point Inn's hospitality. I hear it has an excellent reputation."

"Sorry," I said coldly. "We're full up at the moment."

He made a show of petting Patience. "I think you'll find you can manage one room," he said. "We both know you hold a couple in reserve for possible VIPs." His eyes met mine. "I think you'll agree I qualify."

"Get out," I said. My hand on the doorknob was the only thing holding me upright.

He smiled as he walked past me and out into the lobby. "I'll check in with Reception in an hour," he said. "It would be great for everyone concerned if you had some news for me by then."

I closed the door behind him, slumped up against it. I felt incredibly alone. What could I tell Mike, or Mirela, or—especially—Galina?

I knew what I should do. I knew who I should call. This was potentially, or even probably, a police matter. Julie Agassi was the only person who could do anything about this guy, maybe buy me some time, lock him up (we did, after all, have a shiny new police station with spiffy holding cells) while I could call the magic number, and… what? *Breathe, Riley, just breathe. In, hold it, out. Breathe.*

There was nothing Ali could do from wherever he was; he couldn't cut an assignment short on the basis of conjecture. Warning him sounded like a good idea, but of what? The threats weren't specific enough to act on, and I wasn't inclined to wait around until they could become more specific.

And what was Julie going to do? Arrest Andrew Young on the basis of a conversation he'd had with me? If I claimed he'd threatened me, it was his word against mine. I'd seen enough domestic violence cases get dismissed when the abused partner was accused of making the accusations up. My only bruises hadn't come from Andrew, they'd come from an explosion, which argued powerfully that I might not even be in my right mind, having experienced a near-death situation only twenty-four hours ago.

I couldn't reach out to Ali, and Julie couldn't help. But there was one person who might hold the answers, one person who'd urged me to find out what was going on behind the scenes, and that person was Mirela.

But I wasn't going to her house. Not now, and not directly. Who knew who might follow me?

You're paranoid, Riley, I thought. But maybe not.

And maybe it's the paranoid who survive.

12

If I'd been looking for a quick and quiet word with Mike, I was going to be disappointed. By the time I made it out to Reception there was an argument going on, and it was looking to get worse before it got better.

Elliot was at the front desk. (Maybe I was finally getting the hang of this; his name sprang immediately into my mind. Or it could have been just the first name I thought of.) He was attempting to calm the guy standing in front of the desk, and I saw with some shock that the guy was wearing a National Park Service uniform, which was seriously taking coincidence a little too far. He hadn't bothered removing his hat when he came indoors, which was a breach of protocol but certainly the least of our problems, as he was also pounding the desk.

Where was Wendy, our trusty manager, when you needed her?

Elliot (that must be his name) caught sight of me, and the expression of relief on his face was immediate. "If you'll wait just a moment," he said to the park ranger, who turned toward me and I saw with a shock it was Lucy. Why had I assumed she was a man? Was it the uniform? The air of authority? Was I hopelessly mired in 1950s thinking?

Not the time to delve into feminist theories. I had more immediate problems.

She looked relieved when she saw me. "Sydney. Thank God!"

"Hi, Lucy," I said, and looked at Maybe-Elliot. "It's okay, Ranger O'Connell and I know each other."

She seemed relieved. "I've been asking for you, and he said you weren't here, and he wouldn't tell me where you'd gone."

I touched her elbow to draw her away from the desk; too many people were starting to look interested. Not good PR for the inn, having people in uniform raising their voices in a confined public space.

I wasn't going back into the lounge; Andrew Young and his Patience had used up just about all of my own. I led her through the lobby and out into the pool area; beyond that lay the spa, which I hoped wasn't crowded at lunchtime in August. We sat down in front of a benevolent stone Buddha statue on benches facing each other. "I just don't understand how that happened," said Lucy.

It was a testament to how remarkably busy and stressful my life had been lately that it took me a moment to understand what she was talking about. The explosion. The death of her friend. "I'm so sorry, Lucy," I said awkwardly.

"You were there, weren't you?" It sounded accusing, though that could have been just in my mind.

"I was," I said. I wasn't sure what else to say.

She looked away from me for a moment, and I could see tears glistening in her eyes. She drew in a long, shaky breath, before turning back to me. "What happened?"

"I wish I could tell you," I said.

"What, the police said you can't?"

"No," I said, "it isn't like that. It's just—I can't remember."

"You can't remember it happening? Or you can't remember why you were out there?"

"Both. Neither," I said, none too coherently.

"Are you sure?" She leaned forward. "I need to know, Sydney."

"I know he was your friend," I said. I was a little overwhelmed. My husband had been threatened, I'd almost been killed myself, and I was trying hard to summon compassion for this woman who'd lost someone important to her. But I couldn't invent what I didn't know. "I hope my memory comes back," I said. "It's apparently pretty much fifty-fifty, whether it will. But right now—I don't even remember hiking out into the dunes. I don't remember why I did. I must have been at Cyril's shack, but I just don't remember."

She'd sat back and was looking at her hands. "Did the police question you?"

"Of course they did. They came to the hospital. Local police. And the ADA's office. And the investigators from the park service, I can't remember who they were." With a little luck, maybe we could get the FBI and the CIA involved, too.

"It was the ISB," she said, adding to the alphabet soup, her thoughts clearly elsewhere. I vaguely remembered the agent from the emergency room; even with Mirela talking over him, he'd made an impression. "They didn't suggest… you would probably know if they thought…"

I was genuinely not getting what she was talking about. "Thought what?"

She raised her gaze to my face again. "That you were involved," she said.

I stared at her. I had never even considered the possibility that anyone else would consider *me* a possibility for what had happened. I didn't know whether that was the mark of an innocent person or an exceptional con artist. "No," I said. "No one's said anything about me as…" I took a quick breath, "…a suspect."

"I see." She was pretty unruffled for someone who'd just caused seismic shudders through my world. On top of the other seismic shudders the day had already delivered. I couldn't wait to see what happened next. This was either a very bad movie—or Sydney Riley's life.

Yeah, I know, I know. My life is an ongoing bad movie. "I think," I said slowly, "that if I'd meant to blow anything up, if I'd gone out there with dynamite or whatever, it might be something that stuck in my mind." On top of the whole I-don't-make-it-a-practice-to-cause-explosions thing, it would have taken more resources and preparation than I could muster while forgetting everything about it.

"And yet you don't remember anything." She sighed. "I don't mean to accuse you of anything, Sydney. I'm just looking for answers. I'm not involved in the investigation. You probably know that already. I'm not investigative branch. But Cyril was… he was special, and I'll be honest, no one from inside the park service is going to tell me about what they find or don't find. So I'm relying on you."

Not a wise choice at the best of times, I found myself thinking. Right now I wasn't sure I could deduce my way out of a paper bag with a machete. I was going to have to get a grip if this whole thing wasn't to end very messily. And Ali…

I clamped down on that thought fast. "I can't help you," I said to Lucy, and started to stand up.

She startled me by reaching over and clasping my wrist. "Please don't say that. You can't…" I could feel her fingers shaking. "Listen, Sydney, here's the thing, Cyril was going to meet me yesterday. He was supposed to be down on the beach, there was this place we met sometimes, I'd bring a Thermos of iced coffee, and we'd talk. I was there when I heard the explosion. He was supposed to be there with me. I don't know why he wasn't."

I gently eased my wrist out of her grasp. "He didn't strike me as the world's most rigorous timekeeper," I said. And wasn't that the point? When Ali and I were first out at Louis's shack, I was constantly unsettled by our perceptions of the passage of time. In town, I had deadlines, schedules, appointments, meetings. If you asked me at any moment approximately what time it was, I could tell you without consulting my watch. But out in the dunes, time didn't so much stand still as it was irrelevant. We ate when we were hungry, went to sleep when the sun set. That was all that mattered to us, and we were only there a week.

Cyril had lived like that for decades. I wouldn't have expected him to turn up for anything at any given time.

"He managed," she said, a little stiffly; obviously my criticism had annoyed her. "Cyril always was on time."

"Okay," I said, keeping my voice noncommittal. I didn't have any preference one way or another; there were enough entities investigating this event, they didn't need Sydney Riley putting her oar in. Especially since she couldn't remember a damned thing about what had happened.

"I'm just trying to figure it out."

I took a deep breath. "I understand that, Lucy, and I'm so sorry for your loss. I really am. And I promise if I remember anything, I'll tell someone." I had no idea who that someone might be, but we'd cross that bridge when we came to it. "But I have a lot to do today, and—"

"You'll tell me?" She whipped out a business card. "This is my cell number. You can call it anytime."

"Okay." I stood up and took the card awkwardly. I was pretty sure she'd already given me one. Maybe the print shop had had a sale going. "I'm sure they'll figure out what happened. It just—this kind of thing takes time."

"I know." She seemed to realize how she was coming across, and offered me a tentative smile. "It's just I'd have liked to know what his last words were. What the two of you talked about. Make sure he was doing okay."

"I understand," I said, though I probably didn't. I gestured back toward the pool. "I really have to go now."

"Of course." She stood up abruptly and held out her hand for me to shake. "Thanks, Sydney."

Wendy was standing in the doorway beyond the pool watching us as we made our way across. I let Lucy go in ahead of me. "Were you looking for me?"

She nodded. "Your office?"

Then it was serious, and I really didn't need any more serious stuff today. We didn't speak until my door was closed behind us. "It's Mike," said Wendy.

"What's wrong?" No: not Mike. He hadn't been included in the threat, but if Andrew Young had done anything to him, I'd have a go at the lawyer with my bare hands. "What's happened?"

"He's incandescent," said Wendy. "No, no, he's fine, Sydney, that's not it. But I've never seen him so enraged. We're keeping it quiet, of course, but—"

"Wendy," I interrupted. "Please just tell me. I've already had a really long day. What's happened?"

"Rosa found it," said Wendy. She came and sat in one of the client chairs in front of my fairly insubstantial—and, it has to be said, fairly girly—desk; she looked like she was trying to avoid touching it. There is nothing girly about Wendy.

"Found what?" Rosa was one of the chambermaids at the inn; I had a fairly good grip on their names, perhaps because they tended to stay with us longer than did all the

Kevins. Rosa was from Jamaica, was dependable and funny and smart. I liked her a lot. *Please don't tell me anything bad about Rosa…*

Wendy said, her voice flat, "Drugs."

I stared at her. "You're kidding." I don't know what I'd been expecting, but that was certainly not it.

"In the sofa cushions," said Wendy. "When she was cleaning that suite…"

"The Cargills' suite," I said. The way things were going, it couldn't be anything else. Or anyone else. Now Galina and I had a whole new fresh conversation to share.

Wendy nodded. "Tiny plastic bag," she said. "White powder."

"What drug?"

She shrugged. "Take your pick. Cocaine, maybe. Powdered meth. Special K. GHB."

I held up my hand. "Got it." And what did you want to guess, whichever drug it happened to be, there'd be fentanyl in it as a topper? No wonder Mike was incandescent with rage; he'd just had a death this week, too, and deciding to volunteer for an agency addressing substance abuse while having drugs on the premises… well, I got it.

To be fair, I'd guess that every hotel and inn in Provincetown has at some point—some more regularly than others—had people using drugs on their premises. In season, it's a party town; we're even a stop on the "circuit" of gay men's parties that include heavy drug use along with lots of dancing and lots of sex. And the parties aren't harmless: it's common for circuit party promoters to hire medical professionals to be stationed outside venues in anticipation of drug overdoses, dehydration, or alcohol poisoning during an event.

But the truth is, people on vacation do things they don't necessarily do at home. Much of the illicit drug use in P'town doesn't happen out on the streets; it's a private matter, part of a party or rave or night out. A baggie of white powder wasn't going to necessarily give Mike a case of the vapors, and a year ago he'd have hardly lifted an eyebrow; it was to some extent just part of cleaning up after the tourists. The only odd thing really about its presence was… well, its *presence*: people don't normally walk away from that kind of financial interest—no drug comes cheap—and if they were habitual users, they wouldn't have left the room without first doing a thorough search for their baggie. And in the sofa cushions? Wasn't that the *first* place you'd look?

The presence of the powder in one of our rooms wasn't shocking; what was alarming to me was whose room in which it happened to be.

Which led to an obvious question: did Barclay and Galina Cargill strike me as drug users, much less abusers? Hardly. Was it alarmingly convenient, then, that just as someone turned up looking for Galina, some drugs appeared in the room she'd just vacated? I was happy to put this on Andrew Young's account for sure.

It felt as if there were a lot of factors coming together, somehow, but I couldn't see how they fit. And they were coming at me too quickly. I was feeling a little dizzy.

Wendy was still talking. "He turned it over to the police," she was saying. "I don't know if they'll want to pursue it or not—it wasn't a significant quantity, not like they had anything for distribution, so… well, I don't know. But Mike really lost his shit over it."

"He knew someone who died of an overdose," I said absently. "Quite recently."

Wendy nodded; she'd known. "I don't know where he is," she said. "And that's fine, I don't need him for anything, but… well, it's just that I'm a little worried. I mean, Rosa isn't going to tell anybody, but if word gets out…"

"If word gets out," I said briskly, "then it'll also be obvious that we did the right thing. We located the substance and we turned it over to the police. There wasn't anything else there, right?"

She shook her head. "Rosa would have found it."

"So there it is. Don't worry about our reputation, Wendy." She did worry, and that was a good thing—it made her a good manager, but right now I had weightier matters on my mind.

And I was still wondering if the discovery hadn't been just a little too convenient.

If Andrew had meant for Galina to be arrested, he wasn't going to get his wish. Nothing would tie her directly to the bag; it sounded like personal-use size only; and, perhaps best of all, no one knew where she was. Maybe he'd meant to smoke her out. If that were the case, I was feeling marginally better about things, because it wasn't a terribly bright move.

Wendy stood up and headed for the door. "Just wanted to keep you in the loop," she said.

"I appreciate it." I wasn't going to get anything done at the desk; even if I'd been in any state to concentrate, the sunlight streaming in through the French windows was blinding, obscuring everything in its brightness. Temporarily blinded, I felt it was an apt metaphor. Something far too bright was keeping me from seeing what I really needed to see. All I had to do was—metaphorically, of course—close the drapes to see what I was missing.

But I had no idea where to find the correct cord to pull.

***

Lucy hadn't gone far; she was standing near the restaurant entrance, deep in conversation with a couple who'd apparently been leaving after lunch. Or going in for lunch—but no one fortunate enough to snag a reservation in August was going to dilly-dally about in Reception.

It wasn't Lucy's presence, though, that had my stomach suddenly clenching; Andrew Young, Patience under his arm, was talking to Elliot at the front desk.

I wasn't ready to see him. It had only been—what, an hour?—since he'd issued his ultimatum, and I hadn't even had a chance yet to call Mirela. I took a deep breath and headed over to the desk. "Mr. Young."

He turned to me and smiled. "Sydney! Great to see you. I've just been telling this gentleman that you had a room reserved for me."

Elliot was looking a little confused. "It's okay," I said to him. "Please give Mr. Young four-forty." We don't have four hundred rooms; room four-forty was one we typically held in reserve, just in case. My father had occasionally taken advantage of it. "For one night," I added quickly.

"For now," Andrew said with a smile that felt all too intimate. He was probably younger than I was, though I'm really no good at guessing people's ages, and that smile sent a shiver up my back. There was something about it, something that said *I have you exactly where I want you*, that was more than a little scary.

Of course, maybe that was just me. Maybe he smiled like that to everyone.

Elliot was saying, "All I need is some form of ID, sir," to Andrew and I realized this might be my only moment to escape, when he clearly couldn't follow me. Of course, for all I knew, he might have minions lurking out on Commercial Street to do his bidding, but I rather thought not. He struck me as an independent sort of blackmailer.

And I was out of there like a shot.

***

I hit Commercial like one of the kids who weave their bicycles at high speed through the pedestrian traffic that clogs up the street from May to October; I wasn't going to let this meager advantage go to waste. Breathless by the time I reached Lopes Square, I miraculously found a space on one of the benches and pulled out my phone. "Where are you now?"

Mirela's voice sounded amused. "I am immersed in finger-paints with your goddaughter," she said. "Thank goodness for the speakerphone."

"Take it off speaker," I said impatiently. "I have to talk to you."

There were a few moments when I could hear running water in the background, then a click, and her voice closer in my ear. "What is it?" she asked.

"Galina," I said. "She still staying there with you?"

"Where else would she go?"

That was the snag, of course; there weren't that many places Galina could be, and anyone with half a brain could figure that out. Andrew Young had more than half a brain. "Something's happened, we need to get her out," I said.

"What is it?"

"Long story," I said. "But she's possibly in danger, and certainly Ali is."

"Ali is always in danger," she said. "It is the nature of his profession."

Mirela and Ali are close friends; I think she worried as much about his undercover work as I did. "That's not it," I said. "There's this guy—" How to encapsulate it all in a telephone call? "Never mind, I'll tell you the details later. But Galina isn't safe at your house. Where are you now?" If she was doing finger painting with Lily, they could well be at Mirela's studio, where she wouldn't care what color went where.

"We are at home, sunshine. Do you wish to speak to Galina?"

"No," I said. This was going to get complicated; I didn't want Lily endangered on top of everything else. "I'm on my way."

Franklin Street connects with Commercial Street at the point where Commercial takes an abrupt turn to the left to continue hugging the harbor, making room for the Coast Guard station with its long pier. Perry's Fine Wines is on the corner, and what I would have given to be sipping one of those fine wines at the moment. I turned and went resolutely uphill, chugging more and more with each step.

I really should get a gym membership. I really should.

Mirela's home is on upper Franklin, so I had plenty of time to consider the sorry state of my cardiovascular system before I got there. She lives behind a gate, which might make her safer if she ever locked it. Not that a lot of us do—lock things, that is. In season, perhaps, yes, it's wise; but in the off-season most of us don't bother. That may be changing, and now that I no longer lived in an apartment the size of a teacup it wasn't anything I needed to think about. (Not that I'd thought much about it then: the lock on my apartment never really worked, and my landlord kept the building unlocked, as there was a nightclub beneath me where vendors had to come and go during the day, and customers at night.)

Her front door was open and I walked in, Mirela coming into the front hall—empty except for a table and some of her more emotional paintings on the walls—without Lily; the nanny had doubtless been called. "What is it?" she asked me. Mirela might have the courage of a lion, but she had the protective maternal instincts of one as well. "Come into the garden, sunshine, we can talk there."

We sat at her elegant wrought-iron table. "Where's Galina?" I asked.

"Upstairs," she said, with a vague gesture of her hand. "Where should she be?"

"I don't know." My walk down Commercial Street and up Franklin hadn't given me much in the way of inspiration. "Mirela, did she tell you about something she has that maybe she shouldn't? Or something important her husband left? It's a thing, an object."

Mirela frowned. "She has not spoken to me of that. Only that she wishes his murder to be solved."

"I'm working on that," I said. "Can I talk to her?"

"But of course, sunshine," said Mirela. She looked puzzled, but went into the house and reappeared a few moments later, Galina in tow.

The woman had already been fashion-thin when I met her at the Race Point Inn; now she looked downright gaunt. Even if she'd once been a trophy wife, she was one who was suffering enormously at his loss. She could have already been far away by now, and instead she was sitting here, listening to Lily's temper tantrums and waiting for me to do something constructive.

Well, I'd been a little busy. Explosion, trip to the hospital in Hyannis, threats by a lawyer—and his little dog, too.

"You have learned something?" Galina asked me.

"Maybe." I hesitated. "Galina, does the name Andrew Young mean anything to you?"

She thought about it, then shook her head. "I do not think so," she said.

"I think he was one of the people in your suite the night Barclay was killed," I said. "The man, the one who wasn't wearing a uniform, would you remember him?"

"We did not speak," she said. "I think I would recognize him if I saw him again. Is that what you are asking?"

"Not exactly." I took a deep breath. "Galina, let me ask you this: when you packed up your things from the inn, was there anything special you found, some object, something maybe that was Barclay's?" Besides the drugs, of course; we'd get to that in a minute.

She said calmly, "You mean the key."

"What key?" I was startled; I'd expected her to deny having found anything.

Mirela was nodding. "There is a key," she agreed. "I had forgotten."

"What key?"

Galina said, "I will show you," and went back into the house. Mirela said, "it is probably for a bank vault. I have one like it, myself."

"Bank vault?" I asked blankly. "Do you mean safe-deposit box?"

She nodded vigorously. "Yes. That is correct. But they all look alike."

Galina came out and placed the small, slender key on the table. "There it is," she said. Mirela was right: not only were there no helpful markings on the key, but it did in fact look like every other safe-deposit box key at every bank in the country. In the world, for all I knew. Or a key to any of a dozen other kinds of locks. "This was with Barclay's—um, possessions?"

"Yes. It was not with his other keys. They were on a keyring. This was in his wallet." As though anticipating my next question, she added calmly, "It was not in his pocket when he died. I do not know why."

"But the police must have made an inventory," I said slowly. "Why didn't this stand out?"

"Why would it?" asked Mirela. "It is not really a clue, you know, sunshine."

She was right, of course. There was no reason to connect a random key to anything to do with his death, any more than any of his other keys or papers. Well, the papers, maybe. I hadn't been privy to those.

I was thinking of Gertrude Stein and her famous phrase, "There was no there, there." I only knew there was something there because Andrew wanted it. And it still might not be the key—but I assumed these two had already had conversations going through all the options. The key stood out to his wife; it might not to anyone else.

Unless that someone else was a rapacious lawyer, of course. Who had been with Barclay either when or just before he was killed. Who could, in fact, be his killer.

I took a deep breath. This wasn't getting us anywhere. "Listen," I said. "Here's what we need to do. We need to get Galina out of here. And Mirela, you have to give David the key. We can't drive around aimlessly from bank to bank—and even if we knew the right bank and the right box number—"

"Which we do not," said Mirela.

"Which we do not," I agreed. "Even if we had all that, though, the bank would ask for identification. I think being his widow wouldn't be enough, that sort of thing has to go through the estate resolution, unless her name were on the box too." Once in a while, random bits of trivial information I'd collected paid off. "But you'd know if that were the case," I added, looking at Galina.

She shook her head. "I never saw it before," she said.

"Perhaps it was not his?" asked Mirela. "If Galina did not know it was in his possession, perhaps then it was someone who gave it to him. For safekeeping."

Not all that safe, I thought. But maybe no one knew he was going to be killed. Except for the killer, of course.

I said, "The man who was with your husband, one of the men you saw in the suite, his name is Andrew Young. He is an attorney, and was doing some sort of deal with your husband. I don't know what the deal was, I don't know anything about it." No need to tarnish Barclay further. "But he's a bad man, Galina. He wants me to bring you to him. He knows you have something. I don't think he knows it's a key, but he knows you have something. And I think he could get very unpleasant if you didn't give it to him." And then get forced to try and track down the box? The image of them traipsing all over eastern Massachusetts looking for the right bank was absurd.

But the potential for violence is always absurd until the violence actually happens.

Mirela said calmly, "He knows who I am. He will know she is here."

I nodded. "Yeah, I think so."

"Okay." She turned to Galina. "Go and pack a bag for yourself. We will find a safe place to store you."

We watched her go. "I don't think you can actually store a person," I said.

"It is what we wish to do. We should be honest about it." She shrugged. "There is more," she said.

"What d'you mean?"

"You said that Ali is in danger."

Breathe, Riley. "He threatened him, yeah. He knows who Ali is, he knows he's out somewhere undercover."

"He knows too much," said Mirela.

"This is true. First he threatened to mess him up—oh, I don't know, administratively. Then he made some dark suggestions that agents don't always survive undercover." Something lurched inside me. "I can't take that chance, Mirela. I'm going to have to give him something."

She turned the key in her hands. "This was perhaps an insurance policy."

"Well, if it was, it wasn't very efficient, was it? Whatever he's got in that box—and I think you're right, if he was doing something nefarious maybe he had something on everyone else who was involved, that would be the smart thing to do—it doesn't do anybody any good if it can't be located."

"So there has to be a clue," said Mirela.

I nodded. "So there has to be a clue. And one that Galina would know, if she only knew she knew… if you know what I mean."

"And she will be a better clue than anything David can find out," said Mirela, following my thought if not my syntax. "He will do everything legally. He will need to get warrants. He will ask permission. It will take a long time."

I took a deep breath. "I don't think Ali *has* a long time, Mirela. I don't think we can afford to think so."

She shook her head. "No," she agreed.

"So we have to keep Galina safe and we have to keep her thinking," I said.

"Can she not return to your inn?" asked Mirela. "You always keep a room open."

"Taken, I said drily. "Andrew Young is in four-forty. We can't risk it. Who knows what he knows, he's already pretty much up-to-date on my comings and goings. He's already checked in, him and his deaf dog."

She was staring at me. "He has a deaf dog? And this is important, how?"

"It's not. Or I don't know." I was impatient with her, but even more impatient with myself. My husband has rescued me from potential death and destruction—I'm only exaggerating slightly here—more times than I can count. If I couldn't manage just once to do the same for him… I closed my eyes, trying to keep my heart from racing. *Breathe, Riley. Just breathe.* I had to find the answer.

I *had* to find the answer.

13

I wanted to go get the Little Green Car, but Mirela pointed out, very sensibly, that it wouldn't be that difficult for Andrew Young to see me at the inn if I went to pick it up, and follow. I tried Mike, but he wasn't answering his mobile, so I wasn't getting any help there. I was running out of ideas.

Galina was still packing, and I didn't want to rush her, in case she left something behind that would turn out to be the key. The key to the key, I thought, a little hysterically. I was going to have to get a grip.

"Not in my studio," Mirela was saying. "Everyone knows it is where I work."

"Being famous has its drawbacks," I agreed.

She made a face at me. "It is such a pity, sunshine, that you are not still on your honeymoon."

"What's that supposed to mean? It was when I was on my honeymoon that a lot of this happened.

She made an impatient gesture. "This is not what I mean," she said. "You were safe, out there in that house in the dunes."

I stared at her. Safe in the dunes? Actually… yes. She was right. It was a world apart from Provincetown. Only dedicated hikers and dog walkers, historians and rangers knew their way around out there. Someone like Andrew Young wouldn't—and again, if he didn't know there was a there, there, then he wouldn't think to look. And you could see someone approaching from pretty far off.

I didn't have use of Louis's shack, of course; someone else was out there for their week. And other shacks were occupied… I thought fleetingly of Cyril Stephenson, but pushed him resolutely out of my mind. The accidental (and it had to be accidental) explosion and fire were things I would think about later, when I had the luxury of time, when I didn't have to make decisions.

When Ali was safe.

Now I nodded. "That's actually brilliant…" I said slowly. We couldn't camp out in the dunes, of course; but there were ways and means. And I even knew the right person to ask. I picked up my phone and pressed the right icon, hoping that there'd be an answer.

"Ranger O'Connell," said a crisp voice on the other end. I almost fainted from relief. "Lucy," I said, as calmly as I could, "I need your help."

***

"One hour," she had said, and we were coming up on forty-five minutes, and my nerves were shot.

We were still sitting in the garden. Lily had made a brief appearance, but Mirela decided after giving things some thought that she didn't even want Lily anywhere close to the house and had sent her and her nanny off to the Stop & Shop with a long list—in August, with the crowds, that guaranteed at least an hour's respite, and probably more. And maybe the safest place for her was in a crowd. "If he can threaten Ali, he can threaten Lily," she said to me.

I didn't need convincing. I'd seen that intimate smile, the smile that said *you are in my power*, the smile that said, *I can do anything*, and

I wouldn't have argued if she'd insisted on armed guards posted around the house.

But the cavalry was on the way. The green-and-white pickup truck. The official federal sworn officer. Most importantly, the place Galina could stay.

"I'll take you out to the lighthouse," Lucy had decided once she heard my story. "We're one person light this week, it's perfect."

"One person light?" I had no idea what she was talking about.

"You know how we rent rooms at the Keeper's House?" she asked.

"No." I didn't know what she was talking about, and wished she'd get on with it. I stifled my impatience: she was, after all, doing us a huge favor. *Stay calm, Riley. Don't rush this.*

"The Keeper's House, right next to Race Point Light," Lucy said. "We rent the rooms out, July through November. And someone canceled at the last minute for a three-night stay. That was yesterday, so there are two more nights available there. And no one can access it without an over-sand permit, one that *we've* issued and approved. There are other people in the house, of course, but they're visitors, they won't think anything of your friend joining them."

"I don't know what to say," I said.

"You sure you don't want to tell me more about what's going on?"

"I will," I said gratefully. "Just—later, Lucy, okay? Right now I just want to get her out there."

"Okay," she said amiably. "I can do that. You'll owe me a drink and a story sometime." She paused, thinking. "I'll need to grab a truck. And let my supervisor know."

"Don't tell him—" I began in alarm, and she laughed. "Are you kidding? He'll be only delighted I've filled the room. You're paying for it, of course."

"Of course," I said faintly. "Lucy, I can't thank you enough."

"Oh, you'll owe me for sure," she said and laughed again. She seemed to be finding the whole situation highly amusing. "See you in an hour. What's the address, again?"

And so now we waited.

Galina kept rummaging in her purse and her hold-all—she had about the amount of luggage that we've come to expect at the inn, which meant rather too much—looking for God only knew what. She'd stop, shove bits and bobs back into the cases, then suddenly start the rummaging again with renewed vigor. It was starting to get on my nerves. "What are you looking for, Galina?"

"I do not know! I do not even know what I am looking for!" she said finally.

"Do not worry about it now," Mirela told her. Mirela was fidgeting, and Mirela never fidgets. The possibility of danger was getting to all of us.

I was picturing Ali, somewhere out there, maybe negotiating with some gang-connected slave trader for a shipment of human beings. Keeping the world safe for democracy, as he often joked. And I wasn't even keeping him safe. "It would be with his papers," I said, suddenly, grasping at a random thought as it flew by, anything not to think about Ali. "Galina? A briefcase? Barclay had to have one, didn't he?"

"Of course he has briefcase," she said.

"Where is it? Did you look in it?"

"The police took it," she said. "They gave me receipt. They had to look at all his papers, they said."

"The state police?"

"The ones that work for her boyfriend." A nod towards Mirela.

"Can you reach him? Can you call David?" I asked her. "That's where it would be, Mirela, wouldn't it? Some explanation, some clue to tell us what the key is for. Lawyers are all about paperwork, about records, about receipts. That's where he'd keep it."

"He would not leave it somewhere Galina was more inclined to look?"

I was impatient. "Maybe he would have, Mirela, if he'd known he was about to be murdered," I said. "I think he probably always had it with him, and the clues, and everything, and maybe if he had known, he'd have sent her some kind of message. But we have to assume he didn't know. So it's probably buried in the paperwork. David could find it, he's an attorney, he'd understand what's relevant and what isn't. The police wouldn't know that kind of thing; he would. Call him, Mirela!"

She wasn't happy about doing it, and I briefly wondered if all was well in Paradise. Nothing like a couple of major cases to claim one's attention away from a new romance. Of course, he wouldn't have had the romance in the first place if it hadn't been for the case, so you had to factor that in.

When I can, I try to factor everything in. And I was also starting to enter the paranoid phase of my investigation. Could we trust David? Sure, the Barnstable County district attorney's office would have vetted him, but that wasn't the be-all and end-all of screening. And even if David wasn't involved on the other side, handing him the primary evidence might not be the best and brightest of ideas. After all, he had a career to consider, not a missing husband or a frightened woman. He could bypass us—and therefore bypass Andrew Young—altogether.

I was biting my lip as I watched Mirela find her phone and press the digits. We didn't have a choice. I had to come up with something to give to Andrew, whether it was what he was looking for or at least some sort of red herring to keep him occupied. I had a feeling that, like the character in *Fatal Attraction*, he would not be ignored. And frankly, for all I cared, at this point he could walk off into the sunset with whatever he wanted.

As long as it wasn't Ali's body.

I got up and started pacing, nervously, because I felt if I stayed still my heart would fly out of my body. Mirela's garden is cool and serene; she has plenty of shade trees and some well-tended borders, and in this lovely paradise I was feeling anything but serene. Total waste of landscaping.

Ali, dark and beautiful, laughing in the sun as he tried his hand at fishing, not caring whether he caught any or not. Ali, on a rainy day in the back room of an art gallery, stepping in at the last minute to keep me from getting shot. Ali, finding the truth for my grieving parents and bringing a whole new family into our lives. Ali, those first days I knew him, leaning against his car and watching me with amused eyes, a Lebanese-American who always wanted to speak Italian. *"Ecco, la bella signorina…"*

"Sydney. I am speaking to you." Mirela's voice.

I brought myself back from the edge of hysteria to the present reality. I had to get a grip here. "Yes, what?"

She was still sitting at the garden table. "David is not telling me," she said. She sounded surprised—as well she might, men have a tendency to do exactly what Mirela wants, tell her exactly what she wants to know, take her exactly where she desires. David was either not entirely yet under her spell, or had reasons—including possibly professionalism—of his own to set boundaries. It was a healthy thing for him, no doubt, but inconvenient as hell for me. "What did he say?"

She shook her head. "That it is in hand, and that there are people looking at all the evidence. Including the briefcase. He will tell me if they find anything I should know about." Annoyance in her voice; this was a new experience for her. If the stakes hadn't been so high, I might have been enjoying the moment.

"Did you tell him what to look for?"

"Do I know what to look for?"

I swallowed. "Anything that would identify a bank, and stuff to go with that—account numbers, a number for a box, anything like that? I don't know…" My understanding of finance is practically nil, which is why Mike does all that at the inn. I'd have had us bankrupt within a year.

"He knows what to look for," she said. She still wasn't sounding too thrilled, and I wondered if his days were numbered. Either that, or she'd marry him; there's no middle ground with Mirela.

In the meantime, we had a more pressing problem. "Where *is* she?"

"It is not yet an hour."

But every minute that went by left us all more vulnerable, and it was with an incredible tsunami of relief that I saw the Park Service pickup truck nosing its way through the gate. "Thank God. She's here, Galina, let me grab that suitcase… okay…"

Lucy got out of the driver's seat and adjusted her hat squarely on her head. "Let's get the bags in the back," she said cheerfully.

She turned to Galina, her hand out. "Mrs. Cargill? I'm Ranger O'Connell."

Galina shook her hand. She looked a little dazed, and I remembered that not all that long ago she'd seen Provincetown as a sweet little vacation to coincide with some of her husband's business meetings. Too much to assimilate. "Let's get in," I urged her, and the four of us piled into the double cab.

Lucy reversed out of the driveway, and I spent the next few minutes craning my head, looking around, trying to see if Andrew Young was lurking anywhere. I couldn't see him, but that didn't mean he wasn't there. We'd wasted a lot of time.

We made it out to Route Six and I settled back, breathing a sigh of relief. "I didn't see him," I said to Mirela.

She nodded. "Perhaps he will not go there," she said. I knew she was thinking of Lily, and I breathed a quick prayer for my goddaughter's well-being.

Lucy drove us up to the Race Point Beach parking lot and from there to the over-sand route, and I thought my blood pressure was going over the top as we waited for her to let air out of her tires so she could drive over the sand. Back behind the wheel, she maneuvered the truck skillfully enough over the hills and around the curves that constitute the road out to Race Point Light. She gave us a little of her tour-guide spiel on the way, pointing out landmarks I didn't recognize then and wouldn't again. "I brought food and water," Lucy added as we approached the lighthouse area. "Everyone has to bring theirs in, it's like the dune shacks in that regard. I figured you didn't want to hit the grocery store. So there's enough water to keep you good for now, and a crate of stuff. You can let me know if you need more."

"I can't imagine it," I said, as Galina seemed mesmerized by the view out her window—of dunes and sand, sand, sand. She was clearly somewhere else. "It's good of you to think of all that, Lucy. Thanks."

I'd been here before—there was a tour of the lighthouse they gave in the summers—and of course like everyone else here I'd seen the poorly reviewed but beautifully short movie with Blythe Danner and Richard Dreyfuss; but now, with the day advancing, the lighthouse seemed smaller, somehow, less imposing than it looked from afar. That was fine; less imposing might mean it wouldn't come easily to anybody's mind. And besides, no one could live in the lighthouse itself, and most people didn't know about the Keeper's House. I just prayed it stayed that way.

Lucy pulled up with a flourish and had her door open almost before she shut off the engine. "Let's get you settled," she said to Galina, "and make sure everything's okay here."

I wasn't sure what making sure everything's okay referred to, but it sounded good to me. We all piled out and picked up some part of Galina's luggage and followed Lucy to the restored house—white, with red brick and shingles on top—where once upon a time the lighthouse keeper and his family lived, alone out here at the tip of the world. It must have been a lonely existence, I thought, and I suspected that the walls had seen many a domestic dispute.

These days—since 1972, anyway—the lighthouse was automated, administered by the New England Lighthouse Foundation, and the people who stayed here were well-heeled visitors anxious for the isolation. Like the dunes themselves, the lighthouse and its grounds weren't for those who couldn't bear solitude.

The bedrooms were painted cheerful bright colors, and Galina looked with some dismay at the single bed covered by a thin machine-made quilt.

Lucy had caught the look. "It isn't luxurious," she said, "but it's safe. No one knows you're here. You'll be fine."

Galina nodded without enthusiasm, and we all heaped her bags on the bed and headed downstairs. "I'll show you around," said Lucy, "then leave you to settle in. I have to do a couple of things, but I'll be back around sunset to take the two of you back to town."

Mirela looked like she was ready to call a cab, so I said, quickly, "That would be great, Lucy. You don't know how much we appreciate this."

We did a whirlwind tour of the house and deposited the groceries and water in cupboards and refrigerator. Outside, Lucy unlocked the lighthouse itself. "Go on up," she encouraged us. "It's a beautiful view. The lamp up there is a Fresnel lens. It's been called the invention that saved a million ships. Go and see."

Galina seemed still in automaton mode and went in readily enough; after a moment, Mirela joined her. I leaned against the doorframe. "How did this really happen?" I asked Lucy quietly.

She wasn't looking at me. "What d'you mean?"

"This." I gestured around me. "People don't just give up their spots at the Keeper's House," I said. "Not with such convenient timing."

She looked, if anything, amused. She pushed the brim of her hat slightly higher with a forefinger. "I haven't done away with anyone," she said. "It was an appendix; ask any of the other guests. They got him to Cape Cod Hospital just in time." No wonder she looked amused; all that was pretty verifiable. And why was I asking, anyway? Lucy was going out of her way to help me.

She was still talking. "And I actually was going to use the beds for someone else," she said. "But you got in first in terms of priorities."

"Who?"

"No one you'd know," she said. "A kid who could use a couple days' vacation."

Without thinking, I said, "Your son."

And there it was, a single jagged edge of memory flooding back, sitting on Cyril Stephenson's rickety porch and listening to him talk about Lucy's boy, a kid with brain damage after a shooting—somewhere—that had taken his father's life and his own future.

I could almost smell the tobacco, the scene was so vivid, that one bit of memory clear. Cyril's voice, "Jack? Kid's coming up on twelve. Not as you'd notice, him being feeble-minded from the brain damage an' all."

Lucy and I stared at each other. "You're remembering," she said.

I nodded. "He said he was late…"

"What?" She grabbed my shoulders, none too gently. "What did you say?"

"Cyril," I said. "He didn't know I was hiking out to see him. And I took up a whole lot of his time. And then he finally shooed me away. He said he was late. He wasn't looking at a watch, he was looking at the sun." I was remembering every detail, shiny and clear.

She nodded. "He never needed a watch," she said. "He was always on time."

"To meet you."

"I couldn't understand why he was late," she said. "And then the place blew up and it was too late for anything, anyway. But then I found out you'd been out there. You made him late."

"Wait," I said. "What are you saying? That it was my fault he was in there when it exploded?" I was understanding what novelists meant when they talked about someone's stomach dropping. Mine felt like a runaway elevator. "That could've happened at any time." *Cyril's death can't be my fault. How do you live with something like that?* I had no idea.

Nor did I know why remembering Lucy's son's tragedy had suddenly unlocked parts of my memory.

Lucy sighed, and finally looked away. "It wasn't your fault," she said.

"It's not like someone set off a bomb there," I said, still defensive.

"Of course not," she said, but there was no conviction in her voice.

The panic was there again, and I automatically went through my mantras. *Breathe, Riley, just breathe, keep breathing…*

And them Mirela and Galina had finished their tour and were clattering down the bright red metal circular staircase. "It is beautiful," said Mirela with more enthusiasm than I'd have expected; she must have seen something that ignited some artistic impulse inside. That was generally the case when she got excited about things. She stopped and looked from me to Lucy. "What has happened?"

"Nothing," said Lucy briskly. "That's all for now, all of you. I've got to do one or two things, but don't worry, I'll be back."

"Before dark?" Mirela wasn't so impressed with the lighthouse that she was forgetting Lily.

"Or shortly afterward," said Lucy, and laughed. "Don't worry, girls, I drive out here at night all the time. It's perfectly safe."

Strangely enough, I'd never felt quite so unsafe in my life.

14

Mirela and Galina had gone back into the Keeper's House to sort through her things, meet a couple of guests who had strolled in, and think about what they might find in Lucy's box of food for Galina's supper.

I was too restless to follow. The sun was dipping lower out to the west—because of the way Cape Cod curls around, we could see it set into the water of Cape Cod Bay from Herring Cove and Race Point, and it wasn't that far to the beach, so with nothing much to do except think, I started down the path. Bordering it were scrub trees and bushes of broom crowberry and beach roses—the Asian transplant from a ship wrecked on Nauset Beach in the 1800s that now thrived all over the Cape—all starting to look shadowed and mysterious in the changing light.

There is probably some scientific explanation for why the sun seems to accelerate as it gets closer to the horizon, which of course is a backward sort of way of looking at it anyway, as the sun technically neither rises nor sets. But it was going down with a disconcerting speed, or so it seemed to me. And I knew exactly why I was having irrelevant thoughts about celestial bodies and language—anything to not think some of what I was thinking.

Most of all, I was wondering how we'd managed to get ourselves so thoroughly and almost accidentally marooned out in the dunes on what could become a very dangerous night.

The beach was deserted, which was odd for August—there are always intrepid dune buggy enthusiasts who go at all hours, even use their RVs to camp in certain permitted places—but not so odd when you consider the piping plovers, a protected species that nests in the dunes; all the over-sand roads, or most of them, close while the birds do what they can to bring young into the world. As I watched, though, one pickup truck came rattling along from the north, from the direction of the dune shacks, driving right along the waterline. It stopped a few yards short of the waves lapping at the sand.

A National Park Service pickup.

With a sense now of inevitability, I watched Lucy O'Connell get out and lean against the truck, her arms crossed, looking out over the Race, the place where the bay and the ocean meet, the liminal space so unkind to so many mariners for so many centuries.

What was she *doing?*

I didn't know, but I also had a strong feeling it would be best if she didn't see me. The sun had made its fiery exit but there was still light, and I retreated partway up the path, to where a thicket gave some scant shelter, and I sank down in the sand beside the beach roses.

The sky was still outrageous, ridiculous pinks and oranges cast on the clouds, flung up over the horizon for one last beautiful gasp of a day, but dusk was settling elsewhere, shadows gathering in the dunes, the cries of gulls overhead as they retreated farther inland to their night abodes. Soon the coyotes would be out, and the small rodents they fed upon.

It should have been a beautiful evening.

I looked back at the truck and then gasped as, together, two big, dark figures emerged up out of the water, staggering a little and pulling off their flippers so they could stand, a nightmare come to life, and I could suddenly hear Ali talking. *People who aren't supposed to be coming into the United States have used stranger methods. Not big military submarines, of course; but on submersibles from larger ships, for sure. It's expensive so it's not your run-of-the-mill human trafficking, but if someone wants to come in, it's not unknown.*

Someone wanted to come in.

The three figures—Lucy, and the two men in wetsuits—were pulling on ropes, pulling something big in from the water; a large bag, as big as a trunk, loading it into the back of the truck. The guys busied themselves removing gear—I assumed it was air tanks, diving kinds of things, I knew nothing about any of that—and put those in the back, too, before getting into the cab with Lucy. The cab where we'd been sitting only an hour or so ago.

I snapped out of my stasis and scrambled back up the path. We were getting out of there… *now.* We could walk back to town, people did it all the time. Even after dark. But we were sitting ducks for whatever was going to happen if we stayed at the Keeper's House, and it wasn't going to help Lily, or Ali, or anyone we cared about who was under threat if something went awry. I didn't know if Lucy posed a danger to us, but I wasn't about to take that chance.

It took me only a few minutes to get there, but it felt like forever, running uphill in sand that sent you sliding back with every step. *Hurry*, said a voice in my head. *You have to hurry*.

The Keeper's House was bright and beckoning, an oasis of calm in the night, warm yellow light spilling out of the windows and the screen door. I burst in, breathless and disheveled, to find the kitchen filled with people. People I didn't know. The paying guests.

I grabbed the doorjamb to keep from falling over. "Mirela and Galina?" I asked the room at large, a couple of women sitting at the table playing cards, a bearded aging hippie in beads and bellbottoms, stirring something on the stove. "Has anyone seen them?" No time to explain anything; they must be upstairs. I turned to go up and was on the first riser when one of the women said, "Oh, they went for a walk with their friend. They said they wanted to watch the moonrise."

I froze. "Friend?" I repeated. "What friend?"

She turned to her card-playing buddy. "What did they say his name was? Do you remember?" she asked the other woman.

The other card player shrugged, dropped a card and picked up another one. Nonchalantly.

As though nothing more than gin rummy were at stake. "Don't remember," she said blandly. *She has terrible sunburn,* I thought irrelevantly. *She should put something on it.*

Sydney. Focus. "What did he look like?" I managed to ask. I could feel the cold claw of panic at the base of my spine, starting to move upwards. I would never find them out there in the dunes, not in the dark. I wouldn't know what direction to take, or what obstacles were in front of me. I didn't even have a real flashlight, just the feeble one on my iPhone.

All three of them were looking at me curiously now. "Why, a pleasant sort of man, I thought," said the first card player.

"I don't know," said the hippie at the stove. "Seemed a corporate type to me."

Oh, God. There was only one corporate-type person who'd want to go hiking in the dunes in the dark with Galina. Who could be only yards away and we'd never know. As it often did after sunset, the wind had picked up. Refreshing after a hot day, but it snatched voices, moved them, played with them. The dunes were filled with ghosts that moan all through the night; I'd heard them from the dune shack.

Andrew Young was here.

Breathe, Sydney. Breathe.

I tore back out the door, heading I didn't know where. "Mirela!" I screamed into the wind. "Mirela! Galina! Where are you?"

Nothing but the cries of a nearby coyote pack, the animals' howls sending atavistic shivers up my spine. And then suddenly headlights were raking across me and the big pickup truck lumbered into view, with only one person in the cab.

I didn't think; I just ran to the driver's side, seizing the handle, swinging the door open even before it came to a stop. "Get out, get out!" I screamed at Lucy. "He has them!"

She shut off the ignition but left the headlights on. "What are you talking about?"

I grabbed her shoulder and pulled her out of the cab. I think I would have torn her limb from limb if I'd had to. "Andrew Young," I screamed. "He's here! He has Mirela!" I caught my breath on a ragged sob. "And don't tell me you don't know what I'm talking about! You have to do something, Lucy! *Do something!*"

She stared at me, her face white in the backwash of light as the headlights bounced off the lighthouse itself, directly in front of the truck. For a moment I didn't think she was going to stay on her feet, and I dug my fingers into the flesh of her upper arm. "What is he doing?" she asked—it had to be rhetorically—her voice faint.

"I don't care! We have to find them!"

It seemed impossible. Even over-sand vehicles like hers had to follow the tracks or risk getting stuck in the sand, and there was no sense of which way they might have gone. It was fully dark now, the stars brilliant in the velvet sky, the moonrise impossibly beautiful hanging low and yellow and huge on the horizon. It would give a little light soon, but by then…. "Mirela!" I screamed again, the wind grabbing my voice and spiriting it God only knew where. I was wasting time and I didn't know what else to do.

But Lucy had to know. I turned her to face me, roughly, my hands on her shoulders, and gave her an energetic version of Shaken Adult Syndrome. "Where is he taking them?" I screamed. "You're no murderer! Help me!"

She wavered for a split second, then pulled away from me. "Mirela's in the lighthouse."

I let go of her, reeled around, and flung myself at the door—solid, metal, and my hands were shaking but I managed to wrench it open. Up the stairs, hurry, hurry, just a couple of pier lights on the walls as I ran up the circular staircase, the stairs going on forever and I was almost crying with the effort and the fear and then I burst outside onto the catwalk that encircled the big Fresnel lens and Mirela was there, sitting clinging to the railing, the immense lens above her, her face bruised and bleeding. I flung myself down beside her. "Are you all right?" The words could barely come out, my chest was so tight, my breathing so ragged. "Talk to me!"

She nodded, her eyes wide, terrified, looking at something over my shoulder.

I whirled around. But I already knew who was there.

***

Andrew Young wasn't holding his little white dog; he was holding the limp body of Galina Cargill. And before I could say or do anything, he lifted that body and tossed it over the side, a rag doll, a dead weight. I had no idea if she were still alive, or—if that were the case—even if the fall would be enough to kill her. He was, ludicrously, smiling. "She gave me the key," he said.

"Of course she did. You didn't give her any options." I'd regained enough of my voice to speak. The lens made a ghostly background noise, just under the resonance of the wind, which seemed to be dying down.

Bad choice of words.

The platform door opened again and Lucy filled the doorway. "Where's Galina?"

He half-turned so he wasn't presenting me his back. "Never mind," he said. "We got what we wanted."

We? I stared at Lucy. But I'd known it, I think, even before I'd seen her on the beach. "What's going on, Lucy? What are you doing? Is this about the land development?"

Andrew laughed. "That's all Barclay was interested in, anyway," he said. "Stupid way to try and make money."

Lucy said to me, "I didn't want you to get hurt."

It was all finally making some sense. "Galina recognized you," I said, remembering that I myself had mistaken her for a man when she had her back to me. "She saw you in the room with Barclay."

"I wasn't going to *kill* her because of it," said Lucy. "That's not why I brought you out here. I wasn't going to hurt any of you. You have to believe me. I just had to get the key from her—and keep her quiet for a while."

"Until your shipment came in." I had finally, belatedly, realized what was happening. They weren't smuggling humans, the way Ali had described the submarine-to-shore activity to me; they were bringing in drugs. "Fentanyl," I guessed. Not that it mattered.

Except to all the Cape residents dying of overdoses.

Lucy said to Andrew, "Okay, you have the key? Let's go get the rest of it, get out of here."

There was a long pause. "Yeah, no, I don't think so," he said.

A longer moment of silence, and Lucy shook her head. "What are you talking about? You don't need to do anything to them. Put them inside, lock the door, someone will let them out in the morning. By then we'll be long gone."

"Well, I will, anyway," he said. The Fresnel lens was exaggerating the shadows on his face, first lighting them, then throwing them into darkness; it was unnerving as hell. "Lucy, I don't know if this is the best time to tell you, but I think your usefulness is over. And you have to admit, all the money is a lot better than half the money."

It seemed time to say something. "You killed Barclay," I said to him. "And Galina." Probably, anyway. "Don't add the three of us to it." I took a deep breath. "My husband—"

"—is in law enforcement, will come after me, yadda, yadda," he said. "Let's take that as read. You don't really think I'd threaten something I couldn't follow through on? I had someone in the National Park Service," —I couldn't imagine Lucy didn't hear the past tense— "and I have people in other places, too. Including ICE. He can't come after me if I go after him first."

I wasn't even thinking at that point: I lunged at him, and he laughed and stepped neatly aside and I barreled into the center glass wall of the light itself, nearly knocking the breath out of myself.

Lucy didn't waste time. She might not be carrying a gun at the moment, but she had tools, and just as Andrew was watching me hurt myself, she had a screwdriver in her hand and in one flowing arc of movement drew back her arm and plunged it into his neck.

***

Mirela recovered. Galina and Andrew didn't.

I stood next to Lucy, the startled guests at the Keeper's House clustered excitedly in the doorway behind us, the flashing lights of the MedFlight helicopter receding, the blue lights of the park's law enforcement vehicles staying firmly in place. Not for the first time, I realized how incredibly bright their strobes were, even these, vehicles from the Investigative Services Branch, along with the sole Provincetown police truck because Julie couldn't stay away. I had the headache from hell and wished I could just go home and call Ali.

Lucy was in handcuffs, and still talking to me. "I really never meant to hurt you," she said. "I didn't actually mean to hurt anyone."

"I know," I said quietly. "Cyril told me about Jack." I had belatedly remembered it all, the brain-injured son who required so much expensive care. I wondered what would become of him now.

"Cyril," she repeated, and there was despair in her voice.

I looked at her. "Was it you… did you set a *bomb* to go off in his shack?"

"He wasn't supposed to be there!" she wailed. "Oh, God, I never meant… We'd made an appointment. He was always on time. He should have been far enough away so when it went off…"

"You were storing product there," I said. It was the only thing that made sense. "Did he know?"

She shook her head. "But he would have figured it out. It was only ever supposed to be temporary. But he kept saying he was going to repair the porch, so I had to do something. The stuff we bring ashore—brought ashore—

it's in locked containers. Waterproof. Fireproof."

"That's what the divers brought in," I said, nodding. "The ones you met down at the shoreline." Had it really only been an hour ago?

"Right. We never trusted each other, any of us, so we kept things separate. I had the drugs; but Barclay had the key to the containers. And I kept them under Cyril's porch. It worked for a while, but he was getting suspicious of all my visits. He caught me there one night when I was dropping off a package and I had to make up a story on the spot. It was never easy." She looked at me. "I don't want you to think it was easy."

Killing people, it turns out, really isn't all that easy. I took a deep breath. "But you blew his shack up—even if you didn't mean to kill him, you meant to destroy it. You didn't mind taking Cyril's home away from him. You'd become friends, hadn't you?"

She looked away. "I needed the money."

All the mystery authors write about crime as though it were some intellectual exercise. Professor Plum, in the drawing room, with a knife. The whole "you may wonder why I called you all here tonight" dénouement. Elaborate schemes to cover sophisticated motives. But it's *not* an intellectual exercise: the truth is, it's almost always about greed of some kind. About wanting what you don't have. And about people who will do anything for what they want.

Julie Agassi appeared beside us. She might not have jurisdiction here, but there was no way she wasn't going to still be front and center. "Time to go, Ranger," she said to Lucy, and turned her toward one of the uniformed park officers, guys from the Investigative Services Branch waiting nearby. "Maybe you can tell them your story once you're under caution." One of the Park Service guys reached out a hand to hold her elbow.

"Wait," I said impulsively, and she paused. "Lucy," I said, "you never told me… what was the curse on Louis's shack? Who got killed there?"

"How," she asked blandly, "am I supposed to know? It's all history out there, anyway."

And so are you, I thought.

Epilogue

When Ali and I were first dating, I told him this story:

One day when I was little, I was playing outside, watching the neighbor's cat when it suddenly flattened itself against the ground, its whiskers twitching. I followed its gaze and saw a chipmunk, trembling in fear, but in too much of a panic to move. I jumped up, yelled at the cat—which fled in dismay—and watched the chipmunk shoot across the lawn to safety.

When I told my mother the story, I was in a self-congratulatory mood. "Did you see that?" I demanded. "That chipmunk? I saved its *whole life!*"

***

Ali came home the next night; I don't know whether his undercover assignment had in fact ended or if Mirela had left a particularly plaintive message on the magic number. Maybe he was worried about me. Maybe he'd caught the bad guys. Maybe the planets had just found a new alignment. It didn't matter: he was safe, he was home, we were okay.

That whole *Until death do us part* stuff had suddenly come just a little too close for comfort. Too much, too soon.

If the dunes had taught me anything, it was that life isn't stagnant. That the end of things can happen more quickly and more violently than you'd ever think. That time spent by the sea and sand was precious—but that it could seduce you, too, with its hot sun and lazy afternoons.

I was starting to realize that I wanted a little more out of life than just having tourists say to me, "You're so lucky to live here." That I needed to stretch more, to get away from places where I was quasi-famous, to find out who I was when I wasn't part of this town.

That there was more out there, somewhere, that I needed. To be more than just a person who lived in a popular place by the sea.

When Andrew Young had threatened Ali's life, the only thing I could feel was panic. We'd finally married, finally claimed each other as life-companions; I couldn't lose him so soon after all that.

I thought about Andrew Young threatening Ali's life, and I suddenly believed I could have killed him if it would have protected my husband. I wondered how many times Ali had felt the same way about me, when my life had been in danger. Maybe I had needed that wake-up call; maybe I was getting a little too complacent about being Provincetown's answer to Miss Marple.

We sat alone in the penthouse apartment, his arm around my shoulder, my head nestled into his. Life for one spectacular blessed moment felt calm, the future assured… wherever it happened to be.

"You know, of course," I told Ali with some satisfaction, "that I probably saved your life."

He grinned. "Would that be my *whole life, cara?*"

I couldn't believe he remembered that story, that he was paying that much attention, and I couldn't help but smile. "Watch it," I told him. "Chipmunks are a whole lot easier to save."

Author's note

In the summer of 2006 I had the privilege of receiving an artist's fellowship (administered through the consortium of the Fine Arts Work Center, the Provincetown Art Association and Museum, Truro Center for the Arts at Castle Hill, and a dune-shack advocacy group, Peaked Hill Trust): two weeks alone in the Margo-Gelb dune shack, with no electricity and no running water— just the shack, the sand, and the sea. This was before the common use of mobile phones, so it was two weeks of sheer isolation. I began writing a book then (which would eventually become *Our Lady of the Dunes*), working on a manual typewriter and watching my pages pile up beside me on the desk.

One evening I was walking along the shoreline—the sun had already set and dusk was gathering—when two seals suddenly emerged from the water just meters from where I stood. The combination of poor light and my being so acutely aware of being alone influenced my reaction: for a rather terrifying split second I thought it was people, men. And that led me to wonder what would happen if—the storyteller's friend, that phrase, *what would happen if*—they were really human, and really there for nefarious purposes.

And so I wrote German frogmen into the story I'd already begun, of a young girl sent to stay in the safety of the dunes in 1942. And those swimmers are apparently still haunting me today.

The dunes of the Outer Cape truly are a magical place. They are also unforgiving and wild, and anyone who disregards that does so at their peril.

I've taken some liberties with the role of ranger in the Cape Cod National Seashore, and what that role encompasses, and I hope all the very professional guardians of the National Park Service will forgive the license. Also, to the best of my knowledge, none of them is up to anything remotely untoward. And while Race Point Light Station does rent rooms in the Keeper's House (you, too, can stay there), I did add a bit of a fictional flair to the lighthouse itself. Forgive me: I love my dangerous last scenes.

If the dunes themselves are magical, the shacks are even more so, little Hobbit-houses, some of which seem to grow organically from the sands that surround them, others perched on stilts or many-times-repaired foundations. The shack in which I stayed, built by artist Boris Margo and his wife, poet Jan Gelb (who ran down naked to the sea every morning for a very cold start to her day), has a typically extravagant history, as recorded by David Dunlap in *Building Provincetown*:

Beginning in 1947, Margo was the host of an annual "Full o' the Moon" beach party and barbecue, to which the whole town was invited — and several hundred came. Beforehand, Margo would build an enormous driftwood sculpture, up to 40 feet high. After the rising of the full moon, the sculpture would be set ablaze as revelers danced and sang around it. Music was played and poems were read, by Harry Kemp and younger poets. Though Margo bequeathed the shack to his nephew, the artist Murray Zimiles, it was taken by the government and turned over in 1995 to the Outer Cape Artist in Residence Consortium (OCARC) for management.

As I write this, the future of the dune shacks is uncertain. When the National Seashore was created, the first impulse was to destroy them all and allow nature to re-assert itself; and in fact that did happen to many of them. Eighteen were allowed to survive, with the Seashore continuing to lease them to the families that had either constructed them or "owned" them for decades, on the understanding that the leases would end when the tenants died. In 2005 a 260-page report, supported by the Department of the Interior, outlined the "Traditional Cultural Significance of the Dune Shacks Historic District, Cape Cod National Seashore," which concluded,

"Liquid earth." These were Conrad Malicoat's words for the dunes of the Backshore. And as he and others pointed out, lives constructed on liquid earth displayed fluidity as well, a creative expressiveness, a compliant malleability to a changing fundament. To an outsider like me, the shacks conveyed fragility, a vulnerability to natural forces unlike standard communities designed for stability, strength, and durability. But my seeing fragility was a partial understanding. The simplicity of the rustic shacks floating on or just above the sand on pilings was also a strength. The liquid earth of the Backshore had claimed all three Peaked Hill Coast Guard Stations, each version built strong and solid by conventional standards. Meanwhile, the fragile shack settlement around the stations had

endured. The shacks survived through the constant fiddling of their occupants. The adjustments were unending by the testimony of shack users. And the work wasn't easy, labors of love extracted through familial obligation or comradeship. Yet an enduring life on unspoiled dunes was achieved this way, a demonstration of the potential mutuality of a human settlement with dune grass, unstable sand, howling wind, and pounding surf.

Dune dwellers found meaning in shack life. Living roughly at the edge of society was not a summer project, or a vacation, or "an experience" (like programmed shack time) for long-term dune dwellers. It represented a chosen path through life. The potentials and achievements of dwelling on the dunes over a span of years were unique and irreplaceable, according to long-term residents. Living in shacks on the Backshore was part of a cherished way of life. It meant the preservation of Old Provincetown. It meant the extension of fine arts to new horizons. It meant living close to Nature. And it meant the nurturance of oneself with family, friends, and close-knit communities.

I love that phrase, "the extension of fine arts to new horizons," don't you?

In 2023, it was announced that the National Park Service planned to lease as many as 10 of the structures to selected bidders, with an emphasis on persons willing to pay high rates and maintain upkeep, a not-inexpensive proposition. Current tenants were evicted, and while one or two of them received reprieves after considerable pressure was brought to bear, it seems they, too, may contribute to the movement of Provincetown away from its roots and into becoming something of a theme park for the wealthy.

But that hasn't happened—yet—and so for now you can still enjoy Sydney's escapades in and around what is still unquestionably one of the most beautiful places on earth. Thank you, as always, for reading about her!

I'm so glad you've been following and enjoying this series of mysteries set during Provincetown's various festivals and "theme weeks." I hope these ten books have been as much fun to read as they were to write. For now, I'm going to draw a line under them and focus on some other projects—but I have a feeling Sydney won't allow me to ignore her for long. We'll see what happens!

***

A couple of quick anecdotes: As you already know if you've read other Sydney Riley mysteries, I sometimes place "Easter eggs" in the text for fun. I have several of them in this story!

One is the name of Andrew Young, not named—as you might have thought—for the American diplomat and activist. I volunteer at my local community radio station, and my time there often coincides with yoga classes held in the next room. One day I met one of the instructors, who was delighted to tell me how much her husband loves reading the series, referring to "my Sydney." So when this book was coming along and I ran into her, I said, "You'll have to tell your husband the new one will be finished in a few months," and she said, "Tell him yourself," and there he was! We had a lovely conversation and I agreed to change one of the character names in the book to his. (He didn't know he'd be the Bad Guy, of course!) And, yes, he has a deaf dog named Patience.

Cyril Stephenson was once upon a time a real person, too; my dear friend Edward Franchuk

won a little competition to name a character
that I ran in my newsletter (you too can
subscribe to *Words That Breathe* on my
website), and Cyril, now deceased, was a
friend and colleague of his.

Finally, there's the Easter egg I put in for
myself: "Louis's shack" is of course an
invention from another of my novels, *Our
Lady of the Dunes*, and it was a lot of fun
imagining how the goings-on from that
time—1942—might be remembered and
even distorted in the present. Read it and see
what you think.

If you've gotten this far, congratulations! And
thank you for loving Sydney and her world.

Acknowledgments

As always, this book was the result of many people giving selflessly of their time and expertise, and I'm grateful to them all, but most especially to Arthur Mahoney of HomePort Press. Sydney belongs to him as much as she does to me.

My thanks go also to all the lovely people of Provincetown, who allow me to use so many of their own special selves in my books. Any errors in their portrayal are mine.

Thanks to my wonderful editor (and friend) Bill Bowers, who makes things make sense to me, to Miladinka Milic for Sydney's amazing cover designs, and to Kyre Song, who is so much more than just my web guy.

And many thanks to the AIDS Support Group of Cape Cod, especially to its executive director Dan Gates, who's been extremely helpful.

A special thanks go to those who inspire me to reach, to dare, and to keep faithful to my practice: Susan Lambert, Michele Rieder,

Helen Addison, Marge Piercy, and Indira Ganeson.

To those who contribute in myriad supportive ways to the creation of a Sydney story: Carem Bennett, Mandy Robinson, Pat Medina, Bob Allen, Garr Roosma, Jane McDonald, Grant King, Julie Blackburn. Thank you to Mike Tullio for helping me understand detectives (as if!), and to my beautiful family, Anastasia, Jacob, and Sydnia Czarnecki. For Richard Swanson who, after all these years, still makes me laugh.

Thanks to all the booksellers everywhere, but especially to Derek McCormack and Anthony Esielionis of the Provincetown Bookshop and Jeff Peters of East End Books.

And a big thank-you to my wonderful First Readers: Kimberlee Sams, Dianne Kopser, Corinne Diana, Margo Nash, and A.C. Burch. To the ladies from Jungle Red Writers for their support and inspiration. And to the New England chapter of the Sisters in Crime—well, for sisterhood!.

My gratitude goes out to you all and to anyone I might have inadvertently left out— for sometimes I am a bear of very little brain.

No, not that kind of bear.

About the Author

Jeannette de Beauvoir is a published poet and an acclaimed bestselling author of mystery and historical fiction. She lives and works in a cottage near the sea in Provincetown, Massachusetts, and is a member of the Author's Guild, the Mystery Writers of America, Sisters in Crime, and the Historical Novelists' Association. Read her blog, listen to her podcast, and consider her thoughts via *Words that Breathe*, a free subscription available from her website (jeannettedebeauvoir.com).

Did You Enjoy This Book?

If you did…

- Please share your opinion on Goodreads, Amazon, barnesandnoble.com, Powells. **Reviews sell books!**
- Visit my Amazon page and check out some of my other books.
- Give the book a boost by telling **people about** it on Facebook and Twitter.
- Subscribe to *Words That Breathe* at Jeannettedebeauvoir.com (scroll to bottom of page) for book reviews, short stories, quizzes, free stuff, previews of upcoming work, and more.
- Ask your local bookseller to stock *The Honeymoon Homicides*.
- Make it your choice for your next book club meeting. (I'll even join you by Skype or Zoom if you'd like me to!)
- **Email me** at jeannettedebeavoir@gmail.com.